W9-ATB-358

girl defective

girl defective

SIMMONE HOWELL

A

atheneum

ATHENEUM BOOKS FOR YOUNG READERS

New York   London   Toronto   Sydney   New Delhi

ATHENEUM BOOKS FOR YOUNG READERS

An imprint of Simon & Schuster Children's Publishing Division

1230 Avenue of the Americas, New York, New York 10020

This book is a work of fiction. Any references to historical events, real people, or real places are used fictitiously. Other names, characters, places, and events are products of the author's imagination, and any resemblance to actual events or places or persons, living or dead, is entirely coincidental.

Text copyright © 2013 by Simmone Howell

Originally published 2013 in Australia by Pan Macmillan Australia Pty Limited

Front cover illustration of album copyright © 2014 by Jeffrey Everett, back cover photograph copyright © 2014 by Henry Beer

All rights reserved, including the right of reproduction in whole or in part in any form.

ATHENEUM BOOKS FOR YOUNG READERS is a registered trademark of Simon & Schuster, Inc.

Atheneum logo is a trademark of Simon & Schuster, Inc.

For information about special discounts for bulk purchases, please contact Simon & Schuster Special Sales at 1-866-506-1949 or business@simonandschuster.com.

The Simon & Schuster Speakers Bureau can bring authors to your live event. For more information or to book an event, contact the Simon & Schuster Speakers Bureau at 1-866-248-3049 or visit our website at www.simonspeakers.com.

Also available in an Atheneum Books for Young Readers hardcover edition

Book design by Debra Sfetsios-Conover

The text for this book is set in New Century Schoolbook LT Std.

Manufactured in the United States of America

First Atheneum Books for Young Readers paperback edition September 2015

10 9 8 7 6 5 4 3 2 1

The Library of Congress has cataloged the hardcover edition as follows:

Howell, Simmone.

Girl defective / Simmone Howell. — First US edition.

pages cm

"Originally published 2013 in Australia by Pan Macmillan Australia Pty Limited"—Copyright page.

Summary: Friendship, love, and a mystery fill the life-changing summer of fifteen-year-old Sky, who lives with her unconventional family in a run-down record store in St. Kilda, a seaside suburb of Melbourne, Australia.

ISBN 978-1-4424-9760-3 (hc)

[1. Coming of age—Fiction. 2. Friendship—Fiction. 3. Family life—Australia—Fiction. 4. Mystery and detective stories. 5. Record stores—Fiction. 6. Saint Kilda (Vic.)—Fiction. 7. Australia—Fiction.] I. Title.

PZ7.H8383Gi 2014

[Fic]—dc23 2013032738

ISBN 978-1-4424-9761-0 (pbk)

ISBN 978-1-4424-9762-7 (eBook)

FOR MARK AND WILLEFORD

girl defective

BILL'S WISHING WELL

THE SONG "WISHING WELL" by the Millionaires (Decca, 1966) was as rare as it was weird, and my dad named his record shop after it. The guy who produced it, Joe Meek, was famously bonkers. He had occult leanings and Svengali issues. He heard voices, but he also heard music in a way that no one else did. Just a few years after his greatest success, Meek killed his landlady, then himself, and for a long time his tapes were locked away in a tea chest. Dad had "Wishing Well" on a compilation. He didn't like to admit to this (compilations are cheating), but it meant I got to hear it. The song was poppy and bent. It sounded like it was recorded underwater or on the moon. Dad used to say the only reason he even opened up in the morning was on the slim chance that someone would sell the single in. Every other week he'd get that hopeful, pathetic look. "It's coming," he'd say. "I can feel it in my waters. You'll see, kids. Everything comes in eventually."

And Gully and I would go, "Yes, Dad," but we never believed it would actually happen.

This is the story of how it did.

It's also the story of a wild girl and a ghost girl; a boy who knew nothing and a boy who thought he knew everything. And it's about life and death and grief and romance. All the good stuff.

But first the specs—as Gully would say.

It was just Dad and me and Gully living in the flat above the shop on Blessington Street, St. Kilda. We, the Martin family, were like inverse superheroes, marked by our defects. Dad was addicted to beer and bootlegs. Gully had "social difficulties" that manifested in his wearing a pig-snout mask 24/7. I was surface-clean, but underneath a weird hormonal stew was simmering. My defects weren't the kind you could see just from looking. Later I would decide they were symptoms of Nancy Cole.

At the time all this happened I'd known Nancy three months. She was nineteen and sharp as knives. I was fifteen and fumbling. We met when Dad hired her to clean the shop and the flat. I remember her walking into my room with the vacuum hose slung around her neck, sloppy and insolent like a bad boyfriend's arm. She opened her mouth and all this stuff poured out. Did I know that sharks could switch off half their brains? That the average person farted fourteen times a day? That deep in the suburbs middle-aged couples were having sex dressed as plush toys? And I, who never said anything much to anyone, said, "Bullshit!" Soon enough we were gasbagging and lollygagging, and the dishes didn't even get a look in. Dad had to let her go, but she kept coming around. Nancy's laugh—and I can still hear it—was an unexpected heehaw that went totally against her glamazon appearance. "You're all right, kid."

"Kid," that was what she called me. Or "little sister," or "girlfriend," or "dollbaby," or "monkeyface." Sometimes she even used my name—Skylark, Sky—all in that drawl that felt like fingernails on my back, lightly scratching itches I didn't even know I had.

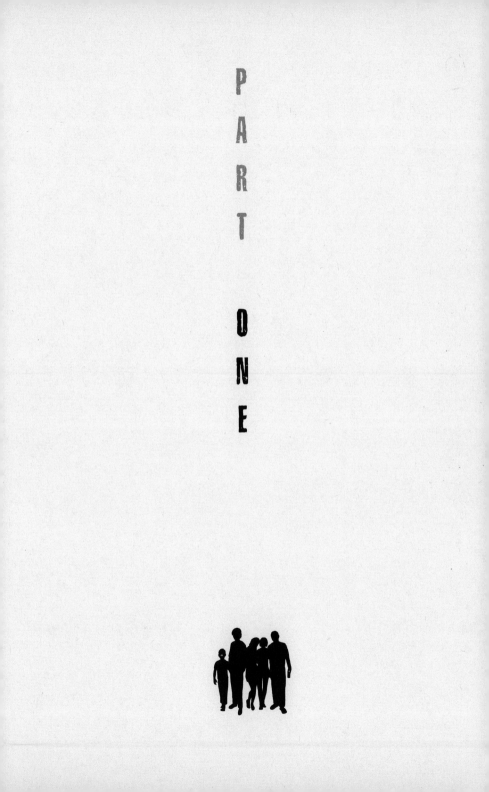

PART ONE

UP ABOVE THE WEIRD

ONE HOT NIGHT NEAR the end of November, Nancy and I were up on the roof. We'd eaten our tea al fresco (Mutha's microwave roast); washed it down with some of Dad's homebrew—nicknamed Old Dunlops because it tasted like tires and made me stupid after two sips—and now we were talking about weird ways to die.

Nancy went first. "Year nine. Richard Skidmore. Killed by a piano."

"Bullshit!" I called.

"Truth. His dad was a removalist. Richard was helping him one day when a piano slid off the truck and squashed him. All the girls were in love with him after that. They wore his picture around their necks and called themselves 'the Girlfriends of Richard.' The crazy thing is, he was nothing before that. He had pimples and he played clarinet, and he wasn't even that good at it."

She took another swig of Dunlops and mock-shivered. "Your turn."

Nancy's "your turns" made me nervous. Her "what

elses" were even worse. I could never match her. My weird deaths were fictional. All my stories had soft edges.

I told her about the book I was reading.

"In the first chapter Freddie Frenger Junior, the 'blithe psychopath,' breaks a Hare Krishna's finger when he tries to give him a flower at the airport. And the Krishna guy dies *from shock*."

"Bullshit!"

"Truth. Think about it. When you stub your toe, it *kills*, and that's just a stub. Imagine a clean break . . ." I grabbed her finger and fake-wrenched it. Nancy let me hang on to it for longer than I needed to make my point.

The roof was my favorite place. It wasn't a roof garden or anything grand. It was more like a perch for stargazers or suicides. We had everything we needed up there: fairy lights and cushions and vintage opera glasses for people-watching. We had the portable record player and records my mum left behind: psycho-sweet ballads by guys with cleft chins, domestic pop by ladies in lounging pajamas.

Nancy put on Dusty Springfield doing "Spooky," so cool and mysterious and infinite. Nancy sang along, trucking her feet and wheeling her arms. After a while she stopped.

"She looks sad. Why does she look so sad?"

At first I thought she was talking about Dusty,

but then I saw where she was staring. The poster had appeared the week before on the wall opposite the shop. It was a stencil of a girl's face, three feet high below a concrete sky. She had black hair and eyes. Her lips were slightly parted, and three fat black tears trailed down her cheek.

"I'll bet she's an actress or a model."

Nancy nodded. "I'm going to ask Ray. He'll know."

Ray was Nancy's landlord. He was fortysomething and worked for the council with a sideline selling books on a blanket near the Sunday market. He called himself an anthropologist, or as Nancy put it, "He likes to watch." According to Nancy, his at-home attire consisted of a faded kimono that was so short you could see his tackle.

Nancy tapped a cigarette out of her packet. She moved on to her second-favorite subject—Her Great Escape.

"There's this village in Wales that got swept into the sea in the thirteenth century. I'm going there. I've nearly got enough money now."

"How can you go there if it's underwater?"

"Did I tell you about the chapel made of human bones? Czechoslovakia. And the hotel made of ice? Finland. I don't want to see the world, kid. I want to see the weird."

"Uh-huh." I bit my lip. I didn't want to think about Nancy leaving. Sometimes I would look at her and almost forget to stop. She had hair the color of orange-blossom honey. It fell in perfect waves around her shoulders. My hair was short and dark and nothing. My look was nothing too. I didn't have to wear a bra, and for that I was grateful. As far as I was concerned, the less stuff I had sticking out and drawing attention to me, the better.

Night fell soft as a shrug. I was starting to crash. Even the palm trees looked tired, like showgirls standing around waiting for their pay. Nancy went back to her plate. She popped a carrot in her mouth and grimaced before spitting it over the rail. She held a potato as if to launch it. "Do I dare?"

"Be my guest."

She pitched the spud. We watched it bounce off the meat-shop awning and splatter on some guy's shoulder. He stopped and looked up. We ducked back, laughing. Nancy found the opera glasses and checked him out.

"He's pretty."

I took a closer look. The guy she'd hit was tall and thin—maybe seventeen. He had black-rimmed glasses and messy hair and vinyl patches on the elbows of his jacket.

Nancy clucked. "He's gone into your dad's shop. What if he robs it?"

"He won't get much."

Below us the sign for Bill's Wishing Well creaked in the breeze. The only people who crossed the threshold were vinyl tragics, weirdos, and wayward tourists. I wondered which category the guy fit into.

Just then Nancy's phone blared so loud it made me jump. She moved away murmuring and came back humming. "That's Federico. I've gotta go."

"Which one's Federico?"

"Long hair, slight lisp, magic dick."

"Don't tell me."

But she did anyway. "You know, like those inflatable dudes outside Crazy John's that jerk every which way?" She rocketed around.

"Is it a date or an assignation?" I couldn't remember the difference.

"It's a date," Nancy said.

I tried to act jaded. I stole her stance, her slang, her style. "So go, lam, am-scray." My smile was unshakable even as I was being ditched.

Nancy kissed me lightly on the lips. She smelled like tea rose and tasted like Mutha's gravy. A weird combination, but it worked.

"Don't worry. It'll happen for you."

She put on her mirrored shades even though it was night. For a moment I saw myself reflected. I looked like a small, dark thing. Like a possum or a raisin. I'd never been kissed, never had a boyfriend. I didn't even know any guys other than Dad and Gully and the odd shop customer. Before Nancy I never smoked or drank; what I knew about sex, you could ice on a cupcake.

We took a last look down just as the guy in the glasses was leaving the shop. He had his hands stuffed in his pockets and a poetic lope and a brooding, care-worn expression on his face. I got all of this in seconds under the streetlight. He paused in front of the girl on the wall. In the dim light it looked like he was part of the poster.

"Hey, pretty boy!" Nancy hollered over the rail. "Want to party?"

He looked up without even the hint of a smile.

Nancy's lips twitched. "Serious boy. Definitely yours."

She said it like it was the end of something, but actually it was the beginning.

RETRO GIRLS

WHERE WE LIVED, IT was never quiet. Once upon a time in old St. Kilda, Victorian ladies would promenade and no one made disparaging remarks about their arses from the open window of an unregistered Ford Falcon. Then came wars and sailors and tramlines and the riffraff bleeding in: working class, immigrants, refugees. Then it was all punks and junkies and prostitutes, and then Money moved in. These days the red light still glowed but only faintly. I could live without the tourists, but there were things I loved—like the palm trees and poppy-seed *kugelhopf*; like the monster goldfish at the botanical gardens and the sad song of the marina boats. The wind played their masts like a bow on strings, and the sound was eerie and lovely and more lonesome than anything I could imagine.

Post-Nancy, I trundled around the kitchen, foraging for snacks. Household was my department. That and looking after Gully: making sure he'd put his pants on the right way, and that his lunchbox had approximately three rice crackers with peanut butter (sandwich-style) and a fruit roll-up (never apricot). He was asleep. I could hear his seismic snores. Dad was still down in the shop, sinking beers, listening to the soundtrack of his youth. He did this most nights. He wasn't a terrible drunk. He just got melancholy. Only occasionally he went too far. Last Christmas he checked himself into rehab. Gully and I had to go and stay with our aunt in the country who made mosaics that looked like monster vaginas. Aunty V was nice enough, but she didn't know what to do with us. We had three weeks of big skies and conspiring cows. Gully was completely out of sorts. When Dad came to get us, his cheeks were rosy and his eyes were bright. He said he'd changed, but he stopped going to AA meetings after a month.

I grabbed an apple and went to my room and flicked through my records. We had record players all over the flat—an occupational hazard—mine was a Sanyo from the seventies that played everything one-eighth of a beat too slow. I put on Tom Rush singing "Urge for Going." His voice was oceans deep and reminded me of old polished wood. He got the urge for going, but he never seemed to go. I played the song over and over until I tasted the sadness.

Sometimes I thought if it wasn't for music, I wouldn't be able to cry or laugh or feel giddy or wild. Music was a valve. Back in the post-grunge days Mum and Dad played pubs and festivals billed as Little Omie. Dad played guitar and Mum played the melodica. She used to empty her spit pipe straight onto the stage. They toured around the country and collected postcards from every stop. I lined my walls with their travels, from the Big Banana to the Black Stump. I also had a picture from an old *Rolling Stone*: my parents at a club, wearing bearskins and grim smiles. They sang murder ballads like the one they were named after, which is about a girl who gets pregnant, duped, and drowned, in that order. Little Omie were going to make it big; instead they made me and Gully.

When I was ten and Gully was six, Mum left us to "follow her art." She changed her name to Galaxy and moved to Japan, where she lived on grants and investments and the kindness of "pointy-headed art fags" (Dad's term). She kept in sporadic contact. I mostly followed her through her website. For her last show she wore antlers and covered herself in umeboshi paste while lightning crackled on a black screen behind her. I don't know how a person gets to that.

Once, I asked Dad which traits I got from Mum. He looked at me for a long time, but he could only come up with one: "Persistence."

Mum used to be a thrift shop queen. She could stand for an hour next to a guy who'd messed his pants if it meant getting to the good stuff. And there was always good stuff. My room was like a shrine to her kitsch. I had tiki dolls and Tretchikoff prints, a pair of rocket lamps, a kidney-shaped occasional table, and a ward-robe full of heart-in-mouth vintage clothes. I wasn't brave enough to wear the angel-sleeve minidress with pompom trim, or the forties black bombshell bathing suit, but I knew their value was higher than money. The clothes were the reason Nancy and I clicked.

A star on my calendar marked August 12. That was the day Nancy opened my wardrobe and almost stopped breathing. She held up a pair of clamdiggers and some Lucite wedge heels.

"Can I try these on?"

Nancy sampled outfit after outfit. She didn't ask me to turn my head. I remember she had on a fancy bra but terrible undies. She tugged the elastic. "Classy, eh? Sometimes you've gotta let your choocha breathe."

Finally she lay on my bed in Mum's leopard-print playsuit, a size too small. She patted the space beside her. I lay down and it didn't feel weird. She said, "I'll tell you a secret: Nancy's not my real name. My real name is Nana, like Nana Mouskouri. You know, the old girl with the glasses?"

I nodded. I knew.

We were so close I could hear her breathing.

"Your turn," Nancy said.

I sifted through possibilities: When Dad was zonked, I'd pour his homebrew down the sink (he always made more); I left nasty asides on the message board on my mother's website (she never replied); I had a shoebox under my bed where I'd been collecting pictures of beautiful people (boys and girls). I could have said any of these things, but when I opened my mouth, this was what came out: "I'm lonely."

Nancy looked at me for ages. "We can fix that."

We lay still. Connected.

Then she smiled brilliantly. "Can I borrow something?"

After that, the pilot light was lit. Nancy's presence gave Mum's stuff meaning. She got it—that everything old was good. And now we were retro girls together. I never dared dream of such a friendship. We listened to old records; we read old books. We watched old movies and filched the dialogue:

"I wonder if I know what you mean."

"I wonder if you wonder."

I did wonder about lots of things, but there was one thing I knew: when Nancy wore my mother's clothes, she looked fucking beautiful.

ANARCHY

WOKE TO THE sound of breaking glass. I sat up in bed, my heart beating like a bird in a box. The air in my room was stale and hot. My alarm clock glowed 4:03. Outside my window everything was still, like a monster god had sucked the world in and forgotten to exhale. Then I heard movement: Dad lumbering about, the buzz of the kitchen light. I heard him clump down the stairs. The front door needed oiling. His voice rose up from the street: "Fucking shit." And he wondered where my mouth came from.

I headed downstairs, nearly colliding with Gully on the landing. He was in his pajamas with his pig-snout mask pushed above his forehead. He pressed his back to the wall and spoke out of the corner of his mouth. "Sounded like a gunshot. I think it's the Melbourne mafia."

"They don't go south of the river. Wait here, okay?"

"Roger. Send coordinates ASAP. *Chh.*" Gully pumped his fist and then tapped the wall behind him, all the while looking around suspiciously. Then he pulled his mask back down over his nose and gave me the two thumbs-up.

Gully was ten, but he looked seven. He was a ninja, a detective, a secret agent. He'd throw a wobbly if I bought the wrong cereal, then seconds later be mugging like nothing ever happened. Lately he'd been getting into Mum's video collection: *Dragnet*, *Joe 90*, *Get Smart*, *Monkey*. He loved Pigsy most of all. If you know anything about *Monkey*, you'll know that Pigsy is fat and sloppy and wholly un-crush-worthy, but maybe it was Gully's role in life to love the unlovable. For sure he loved Dad and me.

It was Mum who'd sent Gully the mask—one of her random, inappropriate gifts. It was made of latex and hair, and it looked real enough. Did she know he'd never take it off? Dad said we should ignore it. Martin family credo: "If we don't acknowledge it, it doesn't exist." But it was there. Right there, over his nose, stuffing his speech and sending us spare.

The shop window had been smashed. Shards of glass sparkled under the streetlight. I stepped carefully over the shrapnel to where Dad was sitting under the neon sign that said NOTHING OVER 1995. Illuminated by the record-cleaning lamp, his skin looked as cracked as a dry dam. Two lines came down from the wings of his nostrils, bracketing his mouth, closing him up.

"What happened?" I asked.

He held up a brick. "Anarchy."

"Did you call it in?"

"You sound like Gully. Yes, I called it in. The glass guy's on his way. The cops, too.

"Exciting," I said. Dad rolled his eyes.

I perched on the second stool. With the glass everywhere and the wind riffling in, the shop looked post-apocalyptic. My eyes traversed the four corners of our kingdom: the listening booth/tardis, the Hall of Fame, the Wall of Woe, and Lifesize Cardboard Stand-up Elvis. He was in his gold suit from *50,000,000 Elvis Fans Can't Be Wrong* and carrying a tray of our custom blank cassettes, each with a little wishing well stamped on the label. They were cute, but they didn't sell. Not much did.

Gully said if you looked into Cardboard Elvis's eyes for long enough, you could see the future, but Dad was only interested in the past. He wore all black and smoked Champion Ruby. He'd seen the Boys Next Door at the Seaview Ballroom. His old girlfriends all had Bettie Page bangs and dug hotrods and the Cramps. He lived in share houses where everything was art and statement—they made garlands out of public transport fines and burned the furniture when the electricity got cut off. Dad's stories about the past made the present look like a painting by a five-year-old with no imagination or glitter glue. But when Dad stopped talking, when the needle came off the record, the past was just the past and the future looked bleak. We couldn't really afford St. Kilda. Mum owned the shop (but not the flat). She had some agreement with Dad that I never understood—I don't think he even understood it—but it meant we could live where we lived, on vinyl and tinned spaghetti, as long as luck (or Mum) would allow it.

"One day at a time." Dad cracked the old AA adage at the same time as he cracked a beer. Ironic.

The police came first. They took a couple of photos, asked Dad a couple of questions, put the offending brick in a plastic Baggie, and then moved on to more exotic crimes. Dad and I waited silently for the glass guy. Over the stereo Neil Young was playing "Cortez the Killer." His guitar whined; it fell down holes and climbed back out again. He sang about Montezuma, the Aztec god of communication, and I was thinking I could use his help. Dad and I used to be fine, but I couldn't remember the last time we'd had a conversation that didn't involve directives about Gully.

He creaked to his feet and snagged another beer from the back fridge. "You don't have to wait up. Go back to bed."

"I can't sleep. It's too hot."

"Did you try sleeping under a damp sheet?"

"That's gross. I'd feel like a pupa."

"A pupa?" His face puckered. "Keep it simple, Skylark."

"The pupal stage is just before a caterpillar turns

into a butterfly, when it's all covered in goop. It's the transformative moment."

"Good name for a band. Pupa. Pew-pah . . ." He mulled it over. "Maybe not."

I started fiddling, moving papers around the counter. I found a flyer for a rally protesting the demolition of the Paradise, the old theater on the foreshore. Dad's old stomping ground. Nancy went to club nights there—two generations hitting the same sticky carpet. I scrunched up the flyer and moved on to the next piece of paper. It was a résumé—with a headshot—I realized it belonged to the guy Nancy had hit with the potato. I skim-read his details. His name was Luke Casey. He was eighteen. Not much else.

"Forget it," I declared. "He doesn't even list music as a hobby." I went to turf the page, but Dad's hand came down like a boom gate. "Too late."

I stared at him. "What?"

Dad took another long swig.

"You hired him? But we don't need anyone. I can work in the shop."

"Christmas is coming. You need to look after Gully."

"I can do both. You're supposed to teach me how to buy this summer." My voice was bordering on whining.

I had no problem serving; I understood the vagaries of the rock alphabet: Van Morrison under M, not V; Steely Dan under S; 10cc before the 1910 Fruitgum Company. But I wanted to buy. Knowing what to pay

for vinyl was more than just referencing the record collector's bible. You needed instinct and experience. I'd
seen customers leave, cashed and dazzled, while Dad
marked up their past 30 percent. I'd also seen customers storm out swearing, after being told their dollar
picture disk was worth less than that. You had to be
sensitive with people, Dad said, because music was
personal. But you couldn't be sensitive all the time,
because that was bad for business.

"I can still teach you," Dad promised.

I stared at him. Doubting, doubting.

A fart sounded. Dad and I looked up to see Gully standing where the window used to be. He had given up
waiting for me. He was still in his pajamas and snout,
but he'd attached his superdetective's tool belt. Swinging prominently were the following: magnifying glass,
talcum powder, soft brush, rubber gloves, and notebook
and pen.

"Don't touch anything," Gully ordered. "I have to
dust for prints."

Back upstairs I still couldn't sleep. I reached under my
bed for my box of beautiful people. I flicked through
them until I found the actress who looked a little like
Nancy. She had perfect skin and a beautiful life. I could
tell these things just by looking at her.

I started to wallow, and wallowing felt luxurious.

Dark thoughts are like stars, or blackheads—the more you look, the more you find. Nancy was leaving for boys and fun and stamps on her passport; Dad had hired some know-nothing, and I was going to have to spend the summer traipsing after my weirdo brother.

Maybe St. Kilda was just a holiday spot gone wrong. The beach was full of syringes, Luna Park was full of thieves, McDonald's was full of runaways, and those streets so prettily named after Romantic poets were just thoroughfares for BMX bandit drug pushers and their prostitute girlfriends.

When I finally fell asleep, I dreamed about the girl on the wall, or rather, the poster of her. I reached out to touch her tears, and when I brought my hand back, it was black with paint, like she was crying right in front of me.

THE OLD PUNK DAYS

OVER THE NEXT FEW days Dad didn't mention the new recruit, and I didn't bring him up either, but the feeling of him lingered. He was the pith in the orange juice and the burned bits of toast at breakfast. He was the squashed sandwich in the back of my school-bag and the snot flecks on the tram seat. I wanted to tell Nancy about him, but she'd gone AWOL. She did this from time to time. I tried not to take it personally. I'd send her countless chirpy texts, about boring school and freaky customers, but sending Nancy texts was like sending dogs into space. Nothing came back.

The Wishing Well was always a good distraction. The new window sparkled, revealing lurking scuzz. Gully and I set about cleaning and polishing and de-stickerizing all the solid surfaces. We put zinc cream across Cardboard Elvis's nose and a lei around his neck and moved him into the window. We surrounded him with summery albums—the Atlantics, the Beach Boys, the B-52s—and then we dragged Dad out to admire our handiwork.

"Pretty spiffy, guys."

"It's going to bring people in," I predicted.

"People!" Dad harrumphed.

"People! People!" Gully could mimic him perfectly.

People did come in but only a few, and what they wanted, we didn't have. It was the same old story. In anyone else's hands the Wishing Well would have done a roaring trade, but Dad was stubborn. He refused to stock CDs. He didn't care about customer service. If not for our regulars, we'd have died in the dust. They drifted in from the outer suburbs: Mystery Train, the sixty-something transport worker with the Dylan obsession; Big Head and Ghost, hapless junkies hawking grade-three trash; Kylie Minogue's Number One Fan (self-proclaimed by hand-painted sign on the back of his wheelchair); two goth hags we nicknamed the Weird Sisters; and the shop favorite, the Fugg. His real name was Ernst Vella, but he was always roiling and swearing—"Fugg this," "Fugg that." He scared the tourists with his beer and balladry. He claimed to have slept with June Tabor, who was folk music royalty and had a voice as sad as evening shadows. She looked fierce and beautiful on her records. I couldn't imagine the Fugg and June Tabor sharing the same air, let alone the backseat of her limo.

Dad priced records, nodding to Lou Reed. Gully decided Elvis wasn't happy in the window after all and moved him back to the counter. I checked my phone. Nothing. Nothing. Nothing.

"Dad," I said.

"Skylark."

"We should sell things online."

He brought his pricing gun down hard. *Thwack.*

"We could set up a shop on Goldmine. It would be easy."

Thwack.

Thwack.

"You're scared of change."

Thwack.

"It's not safe," Dad said.

"What do you mean 'not safe'?"

He put the pricing gun down and looked at me. "Say I get you kids fixed up with the Internet. Next thing I know, some pervert from Oslo's got you on a slab. Or is selling your . . . bits to China. I'm informed. I read the papers."

I laughed. "You don't. You read *Mojo*."

Dad snapped his fingers. "The cannibal couple. You can't tell me that would have happened without the Internet."

"You're ridiculous."

Thwack.

Gully was watching our spat through two spy holes he'd cut out of the cover of *Record Collector*. He lowered the magazine. "No one's going to eat me."

"You're ridiculous too," I muttered.

A police officer came in. I saw red hair against

the blue uniform. Brown lipstick. She approached the counter with a strange smile on her face. Dad's expression mirrored hers. He tugged his jeans up and patted down his hair. Gully, thrilled to see a law enforcement officer at close range, started hissing into his fist. I adopted an expression of nonchalance, but the lady cop only had eyes for Dad.

Her voice was high with a touch of tease. "Is that Bill Martin?"

"Is that Evil Eve Brennan?" Dad's cheeks had gone pink.

"*Constable* Eve Brennan to you."

They gazed at each other for a beat without speaking, and then Dad opened his mouth. "Fuck me. How long have you—"

"Four years. Crazy, huh?"

"You look good in uniform."

Constable Eve Brennan glanced from Dad to me and Gully. She didn't flinch at the pig snout. A good sign.

"Are these your kids?"

"Yes. Skylark and Seagull. Their mother liked birds."

"How is Gail?"

"Galaxy."

"Are you still . . . ?"

"NO!" Dad coughed. "No, no. Divorced."

Evil Eve and Dad worked the smiles, and it was all Gully and I could do to clock the pheromones fizzing like fireflies around us.

"Evie and I used to hang out," Dad told us. "In the old punk days. She had a mohawk then."

The lady cop rejigged her hat and set her face to serious. "I heard you had some trouble." She jerked her head toward the window. "I'm just following up."

Dad let out a puff of air. "So long ago, I forgot all about it."

"It was the end of school. Could have been muck-up day antics. Silly season. We're canvasing traders. Do you remember anything unusual?"

Gully pushed forward. "I dusted for prints," he reported. "The boys at the lab are flummoxed."

Evil Eve's lips wavered. *Don't laugh,* I thought. But she didn't. She just waited. Gully was tracing the air, skywriting. He blurted, "The Bricker was in a white Jeep. Don't ask me to reveal my sources. It will all be in my memo. I'll send you a copy."

"Great." She smiled again, unruffled. Then she squinted at him. "Do you want to be a police officer?"

Gully was affronted. "I'm already a detective."

Eve fixed back on Dad. "Do you have any security? Cameras, an alarm?"

"'Fraid not."

"He's analog," I said. It came out sounding snarky.

"You can get video cameras, Bill." The way she said "Bill," all familiar, made me think, *I bet they did more than just hang out.*

Evil Eve gave Dad a card. "Call me if anything comes

to you." And then she walked out slowly. Before Gully or I could say anything, Dad turned the key on the till. It made a colossal noise as it spat out the end-of-day strip.

I snatched up her card. "Was she your girlfriend?"

Dad gave me an enigmatic smile.

"She likes you," I said.

"Affirmative," Gully chimed in. "She was leaning into you. That's a tell."

Gully was big on tells. His most noted body language giveaways included shifty eyes; hands touching face, throat, mouth; fingers tugging on earlobes; scratching neck; excised pronouns; deployment of monotone; delayed physical manifestations of emotion; and adjunct random observations.

"Get away," Dad grumbled. "Go fix dinner."

He shooed us out but not before putting on the Sonics, and that was a tell too. Their bam-bam garage punk being exactly what you would play if you didn't want to think, if your insides were jumping and your synapses were firing all over the place. I went upstairs shaking off the shiver that was *my* tell. Things were changing. Dad crushing on a cop? Life was about to get another layer.

Memo #1

Memo from Agent Seagull Martin
Date: Saturday, November 29
Agent: Seagull Martin
Address: 34 Blessington St., St. Kilda,
upstairs

POINT THE FIRST:
On Thursday, November 27, at
approximately 0400 hours an
unknown vandal—code name
Bricker—threw a brick through the
window of esteemed record shop Bill's
Wishing Well, 34 Blessington St., St.
Kilda (est. 1999).

POINT THE SECOND:
Bricks were also thrown through the
windows of Ada's Cakes and Bernard
Levon, Tax Accountant.

POINT THE THIRD:
Asif Patel, proprietor, 7-Eleven, and
Ernst Vella, street poet and luminary,
both observed a white Jeep doing
"blocks."

**POSSIBLY RELATED FROM *PORT PHILLIP LEADER*
NEWSPAPER:**
– Two women egged on Vale St.
– Police concern over increase in
muck-up day antics
– Eli Wallace, 78, camping outside
the Paradise Theater, protesting its
imminent demolition

PROFILE
The Bricker is under twenty—most
likely male and in a high socioeconomic
bracket. He has sociopathic tendencies
and a nihilistic, destructive attitude.
He is possibly a high school graduate or
friends of a high school graduate.

ACTION
Crime scene dusted.
Contact council for list of Jeeps
registered to local area.
Research CCTV unit for shop (video).
Info-share with SKPD via Constable
Eve Brennan.

FAMILY STICKS TOGETHER

THIS IS HOW IT was with Dad: I knew he loved me, but Gully was the true star of his heart. Sometimes I'd see Dad look at my brother and feel the acid tang of jealousy in the back of my mouth. I'd flash on Gully at four saying, "I'm a boy and Dad's a boy, but Sky is a *girl*." And I'd feel cursed and isolated and defective.

Gully's weirdness had always been there. I'd lost count of the times he'd come home from school with a "retard" sign stuck to the back of his jumper. Last year Derek Digby, the scourge of grade six, had a mission to make Gully crack. Because Gully refused to. Despite head flushings, stolen lunches, and sucker punches, Gully just acted like Derek was a bump in the rug he had to step over. One day Gully came home with a spectacular bruise on his cheek. It was my job to walk Gully to and from school. The one day I didn't was the day they got him. I could tell by his uneven footfall that something was wrong. Dad was in the kitchen making spaghetti. When he saw Gully's face, he dropped the pot. The water scalded his bare feet, but he didn't even register this because all his feeling had gone to my brother.

That night Gully wrote his first memo. He documented everything he remembered about the attack:

> POINT THE FIRST: The attackers had
> calamari breath.
> POINT THE SECOND: One of them was wheezy
> and kept puffing on an inhaler.
> POINT THE THIRD: Another didn't want to
> kick me—his friends called him a pussy.
> POINT THE FOURTH: They all had
> skateboards.

The next day Dad and Tony Trucker, a regular who loved Merle Haggard and was built like a Hummer, went down to the chip shop and found Derek and two of his "boys" eating calamari rings and kicking their boards around. I don't know what Dad and Tony did, but Derek never bothered Gully again.

"We're Family," Dad said. "And Family sticks together."

After the spectacular bruise, we had a visit from a social worker. Paul Bean had a kind face but defeated eyes. He said no to the beer (it was ten thirty in the morning) and delicately moved the festy stacks of *Mojo* and *Record Collector* so that he could sit in the broken seat of the wicker chair. He asked halting questions about health and family history. He gave Dad information sheets and a speech about how the "functional family unit" thrives on "routine" and "structure" and "support networks."

Dad had *Sgt. Pepper's* on the record player. He must have seen the glint in Paul's eye, because he cranked it up and by the time "She's Leaving Home" had made us all choky, we knew that Paul Bean the Social Worker had been named after Paul McCartney the Beatle. That in 1964 Paul Bean's mother had snuck into the Southern Cross Hotel, where the Beatles were staying on their first Australian tour. That she had stood in the lift with Paul McCartney and never fully recovered. Dad put *Sgt. Pepper's* (near mint, Australian pressing) back in its cover and into Paul Bean's hand, and we never saw him again.

At breakfast Dad was a happy man. "Sky, my girl," he said, crunching his toast in triumph. "Always remember, if you can get a man talking about the thing he loves, you can make him forget the thing he came for."

Dad always told the truth. And he always had a way to say it that made it seem less scary than it was. When I asked him what he thought Paul Bean wanted, he said, "Oh. Just to see how you kids are doing. People can get funny when the mother is out of the picture."

Mum left in the winter, when everything was dull and gray. Gully and I had our breakfast porridge and trotted off to school with our cheese-and-pickle sandwiches in recycled brown paper bags, and the day was the day was the day. When we came home, she was gone. She'd left notes for each of us, pinned them to the mantel like Santa stockings. Mine said this:

Become the change you want to see in the world. Skylark,

I don't remember if it was Gandhi who said that or Uma Thurman. I used to think words become yours, ideas become yours, as soon as you use them. Lately I'm thinking about: how it works that Gully's still wetting the bed; how you've turned out to be this dad-happy whirl of a girl and you don't need me; how your father is. I don't like his beard, do you? And I never liked Nick Cave. I need you to know that this isn't good-bye, but I want to live the kind of life where my thoughts and ideas come first so that I know they are truly mine. I am reconciled to the fact that you will hate me. I hope not forever. Hug Gully every day for me. I know he can't stand it, but do it anyway. There's a reason I named you two after birds, you know. Tell your father to buck up and stop crying. He was always a better mother than I was.

Love,
Galaxy

Mum's letter had infinite creases from being folded and refolded and scrunched and pitched and saved. I couldn't bring myself to throw it away. Mum was glamorous and heartless, but the weird thing was, she was right. We coped. We were okay. Better than okay, we were fine. Dad stopped crying. Gully let me hug him. For a while there I couldn't stop. He drew a portrait of us that Dad ended up framing: three round heads with smiles that went outside the lines.

RITUAL DAYS

MY BEDROOM WINDOW LOOKED straight into the Conscious Body Yoga Studio, where the lights were always on and the blinds were always up. At night it was like a version of heaven with gleaming floorboards and birds of paradise and the mirror reflecting infinite space, but from six in the morning it was butt row. When I woke up on Sunday morning, the nine-o'clock class was doing the downward dog. I kicked off my covers and copied the moves until my wrists buckled, and then I got dressed.

Sundays were ritual days. Dad opened late so we could have a family breakfast. We'd pick up coffee and toasties and take them down to the gardens near the market. Every week was the same. At a certain point under a certain palm, Dad would fix on the white tents and sigh, "St. Kilda really used to be someplace."

The market started at the laughing mug of Mr. Moon, the clown-face entrance to Luna Park, and wound upward past art deco flats and the posh hotel and the old Esplanade Hotel, site of untold puke-ups and hookups. The tourists came in droves and Birkenstock sandals. They had no sense of personal space; it was as if they were *designed* to bump breakfast out of you or trip your rhythm by tramping on the backs of your flip-flops. They dawdled and dithered over whether to drop coin for a hand-painted boomerang or a sheet-metal mermaid or a five-minute massage or their name on a grain of rice.

We found our bench opposite the fountain and sat and imbibed. Seagulls squawked and the sun scattered stars on the asphalt. Behind us the Scenic Railway rattled its first go-round, the volley of screams rocketing down. Gully checked his watch. He held his fist as if it was a walkie-talkie and crackled static into it. "*Chh.*" Then he unhooked his notebook, pushed his snout up to his forehead, and began the meeting:

"Date: November 30. Time: 0947. Location: O'Donnell Gardens. House Meeting actioned."

Dad and I wore matching flat smiles. The house meetings were Dad's idea, a way of keeping us in check, but Gully had taken over. Now they were less about us and more about crime-fighting. Gully's focus was unswerving.

"Item: Does anyone have any questions about my memo?"

"Nope," Dad said. I shook my head. I had the opera glasses on a string around my neck. I was itching to use them. Past the fountain Ray would be setting up his blanket of books. Some days Nancy sat with him. I kept my eyes open.

"Item: CCTV. I have researched some models, and this is the one we should buy." Gully flung a piece of paper at Dad, who caught it and frowned.

"Drago says he might have something."

Gully shook his head. "That means inferior product."

Drago was a fence. He "acquired" stolen goods and moved them on.

Dad mimicked Gully. "Item: We have a new staff member."

Gully's eyes popped and then narrowed.

"Name, rank, serial number," he demanded breathlessly.

"His name's Luke. It's just for Christmas. Don't get excited."

But Gully was beside himself. He knee-walked over to Dad and bobbed around him. "Where's he from? What are his credentials? When's he starting?"

Dad lifted his hand, spread his fingers, and made a cage over Gully's face.

"South Australia. None. Soon." He pushed lightly. Gully sat back down.

"How soon?" I asked.

Dad chewed on his toastie and stared up at the sky as if he was trying to memorize the precise location of clouds. "Next week."

In front of the fountain the Fugg navigated his shopping trolley with the beer-can train. He positioned the green milk-crate podium and started coughing and gurgling, which was a prelude to poetry. Gully fixed his snout back over his nose. "I'm going to give Ernst a memo." He scrambled to his feet and raced over to the Fugg.

Dad gazed after him. "I guess House Meeting's over."

I didn't reply. A bud of annoyance was starting to bloom. I had hoped Dad had forgotten about the new recruit, recognized it as a bad idea. I said, "What makes you think this guy's going to be any different from the last?"

"Just a feeling," Dad said. "You'll like him, Sky."

"I don't want to like him." I stood up and made my way to the small gathering at the foot of the Fugg, who was wobbling on his crate and reciting a poem about the moons of Jupiter.

The market was starting to swell. I scanned the crowd through the glasses: the fat girls in skinny jeans, the caftan women and knee-socks men, the backpackers with their morning beers—you could always pick the Poms showing skin at the merest hint of sunshine. I checked Ray's again and my heart skipped. Nancy was there. She was wearing a burnt-orange pinafore with gladiator sandals and sunglasses that would have put Jackie O. to shame. I ambled over, trying to look casual, feeling anything but.

"Hey, girlfriend. We were just talking about you."

"No," Ray corrected her. "We were talking about Mia Casey."

"Who's Mia Casey?" I asked.

Nancy winked. "The girl on the poster. Ray knew her."

I waited for Ray to elaborate, but he sighed and bent over to pick up a book; his jeans dropped, revealing ample crack. I whispered to Nancy, "The moons of Jupiter."

She giggled. "Let's walk."

LIFE LESSONS

WE WOUND UP ON a patch of green on the Lower Esplanade. Across the road sat the Paradise, all peeling walls and potbellied gargoyles and promises forsaken. A man was camped on a fold-up chair out in the front. He had a blanket over his lap, and a hand-painted sign: SAVE THE PARADISE FROM THE GREASY PALMS OF MONSTERS. I figured he was Eli Wallace from Gully's memo. I went to point him out to Nancy, but she had already started giving me the specs about the mystery girl.

"Ray said she went to a party Christmas Eve. Next day some guy walking his dog found her floating in the canal. She was only seventeen. It was in the papers. You don't remember?"

I didn't want to tell her about Dad and rehab, so I just shook my head.

"Ray said she was a party girl. That's Ray-speak for hooker."

Nancy was an authority on prostitutes. She said they charged thirty for a hummer and eighty for a throw, and most of it went up their arms. They were stupid, she said.

They should have been playing the stock market. I knew their streets: Vale and Gray and Greeves, the cul-de-sacs around the gardens. The girls I noticed were never as flashy as on TV movies. Some were decrepit, but some looked younger than me. They could have been waiting for a lift home from working a shift at Macca's. From the tram I'd see my bored expression reflected in their faces, and wonder what set of circumstances meant I was off to school while they were off to do what they were going to do.

Nancy lit a cigarette that turned out to be a joint. The acrid smoke filled the air and made me nervous. I took a drag for show, but my cough gave me away.

"Oops," Nancy said. "I'm corrupting you again."

"I don't mind."

And I didn't mind the burning in my throat, or the dizzy hit that followed. I stretched my legs out and we lay down. The sky was vast and blue. The fresh-mowed grass felt yeasty under my thighs. I was thinking about Mia Casey, and then I started thinking about Ray and his kimono. Naked Ray, skin folds and rashes. I started to laugh. I didn't stop for ages. Nancy joined her hands and flexed her fingers. She rolled her neck like a boxer. "Want to go out Friday night?" She made it sound like a challenge. "I mean *out* out. You can stay at my place. Ray won't mind."

"Dad would never let me stay over."

"What's his problem? Ray's okay." Her eyes slid sideways, meaning he definitely wasn't.

"We'll tell him we're going to the movies."

"I'm a bad liar."

"I'll lie for you. It's in the details." She was silent for a moment. Then: "Your turn."

The familiar prickle of anxiety soon passed. For once I had news. "Remember that guy you hit with the potato?"

"The pretty one?"

I nodded. "Dad's hired him. Why, I do not know."

Nancy scoffed, "Bill the Patriarch. He wants a son to pass his knowledge down to. Gully's not up to the job. You better keep your eyes open."

"He always does this and it's always a mistake." I told her about the other surrogates: the one who had elaborate phone fights with his mother; the one who smelled like Subway; the one who couldn't stop staring at Carly Simon's nipples on the cover of *No Secrets.*

"At least this guy's cute," Nancy offered. She turned on her side. She was sitting so close to me I could see her pores. "You should jump him. It'll give you the upper hand. And it will piss your dad off."

I laughed.

"You like that idea?" Nancy squeezed my cheek like an Italian mama. "Monkeyface, what are you gonna do when I'm gone? Who's going to give you life lessons?"

"I don't know." She was looking at me intently, and my face felt hot. I had a shock of yearning, wishing that I *was* Nancy. The feeling was sharp and it carried a shadow. I was always on the edge of something that was never going to happen.

"Listen," Nancy went on. "You can get anything you want from a guy. Most guys think about sex ninety-nine percent of the time. It's like the way the sea is—wave after wave. You don't have to do anything to make a guy think about sex. He's already thinking it. The patriarchy, kid. The only thing we've got over them is the choocha." She pointed south with both hands and grinned like a maniac.

"I don't want anything from Luke," I said.

"Dollbaby," Nancy drawled. "You don't know what you want."

We meandered back to Dad and Gully. I felt stoned. I couldn't muster up enough saliva to swallow my smile. I tried to keep a poker face while Nancy told Dad all about the Joan Crawford movie at the Astor on Friday night and how she had to, had to, *had to* take me. "Really, it's educational."

Dad had that look. He liked Nancy, but he didn't trust her.

I held my breath.

"We'll see," he said.

ASK ME ANYTHING

SUMMER ALWAYS KING-HIT me. One minute I'd be fully clothed and comfy; the next I'd have to think about tank tops and body fuzz. I dreamed of cold places: England, Tasmania, Alaska. But I knew they were only dreams. I was not like Nancy. I was a Martin, a resident bird. I barely even left the suburb. If I'd made friends at school, the prospect of Nancy mightn't have been so alluring. But I didn't fit in at school; I couldn't bring potential friends home. My dad was a boozer, my brother was a freak. It was safer to keep to myself.

I sweated through the first week of December. School was hot and noisy and endless. I drifted from class to class like a sea cow. All I wanted to do was lie under a tree or float away in a rubber dinghy. All week I kept seeing posters of Mia Casey. She was on the tram stop, outside the milk bar, on telephone poles. Just her face and nothing else. I had a second dream about her: In the dream she was lying below the surface of the water. Her dark eyes were open. She smiled at me, and a fish swam out of her mouth.

Friday lunchtime I surrendered to the pull of the

library, staking my usual computer. I checked my e-mails and Goldmine and ended up on Mum's website.

Galaxy Strobe is dead!

I gasped. Then recovered. My mother was not dead—the headline was just a teaser for her latest show. A GIF showed a close-up of her face. She had two black eyes. A line of blood crawled down from her right nostril and then crawled back up again.

Down and up, down and up.

A black box popped up on the screen. *Ask Me Anything!*

I typed, *Do you ever miss your children?* And hit return. I imagined Mum reading my message. Her forehead would crumple; her heart would sink like a bag of boulders in a lake. It would dawn on her that her famous life was a crock. Her audience was nothing compared to her flesh and blood. She'd leave Yanni, her Greek collaborator, just as she'd left us. A note on a mantel, an acre of stuff. He would cry hot, salty tears over her abandoned costumes. . . .

I snapped back to reality. It was more likely Mum wouldn't even get to read my message. Yanni was also Mum's moderator, protecting her from trolls and spammers. With two clicks on the keyboard he would delete me. Gone.

Quinn Bishop had the computer next to me. She was the year-ten pariah, a surly, goth bitch who'd sooner sit on you than look at you. She was in the gifted stream and was famous for throwing a chair through the science lab window. Quinn was big, both ways, and there was something bulldog-ish in her countenance. From the corner of my eye I checked her out: her hair (blue streaks on black); her Bad Brains T-shirt over her school dress; her spiked metal bracelet that looked like a pigeon deterrent. She swiveled to face me, glaring murderously, but her face changed when she saw what was on my screen.

Quinn drew herself up. "Galaxy Strobe is awesome."

"She's not awesome. She's a bitch." The words flew from my mouth. "She's my mother."

Quinn stared from the screen to me. "I can see how she might be."

"What—my mother or a bitch?"

Her lips curled into a smile. "Both."

Feeling brave, I scooted my chair next to Quinn's and checked out what was on *her* screen. She kept her finger on the cursor, scrolling a stream of photos of people partying or fighting—it was hard to tell. There were band photos, dizzy lights, mad faces, a naked girl in a horse's head, a singer bent backward like Iggy Pop. I could feel Quinn watching me, testing to see if I was shockable. I could sense her smiling. I wanted to turn back. Then she shifted, blocking my view, and put her earplugs back in. A lost feeling came over me. Everything went quiet, just the echo of Quinn's music and the air conditioner groaning like some mythical beast. I minimized my mother, and another face floated up in my mind: dark eyes, dark hair, three black tears . . . My fingers hovered and then, as if they had a mind of their own, they typed "Mia Casey" into the search engine.

There was an Associated Press article and a photo. The photo was in color, and color made all the difference. Mia looked real. She was pretty—not crazy-pretty like Nancy, but she looked warm, like you could tell her anything and she wouldn't laugh. I stared at her image for a long time, and then I printed the page and read it over and over as if that could change the facts:

Teen Drowned After Drinking

St. Kilda, Victoria (AP)

An Adelaide teenager who drowned in the St. Kilda canal had a blood alcohol level twice the legal limit for driving when she died. St. Kilda Police say there's no evidence of foul play in the death of 17-year-old Mia Casey of Burnside, SA. On the night in question Casey was seen at the Paradise Theater and walking along the Lower Esplanade. Witnesses recalled her uncommon outfit: bare feet, a silver dress, and a crown of flowers. It is believed she became disoriented by alcohol and fell into

the canal. Mia Casey had been staying at
no fixed address in the St. Kilda area since
November. She is survived by her parents
and brother, Lucas.

It hit me slowly and spread like fire. I sat staring at the page in a dunce's trance. Lucas Casey. *Luke.* Dad's new employee was Mia Casey's brother.

The bell rang. Quinn leaned over me; she checked out what I was reading and made a snorting sound.

"She got gypped," Quinn said.

I looked at her. "What do you mean?"

But it was too late. She'd put her buds back in and had signed off on our sorry excuse for a conversation. Quinn picked up her bag and clomped out of the library in her storm-trooper boots. I followed her out to the bright sunlight. Bodies zombied down the corridors to the next class, but suddenly I couldn't bear the thought of being indoors. I lay on the scratchy turf with the sunlight bathing my skin. Mia and Luke's faces floated before me, shimmering like a heat haze. I folded the article into a tiny square and tucked it into my sock, where it chafed for the rest of the day.

THE RED SHOE IS IN THE GRASS

AT THREE THIRTY I negotiated the maze of group-huggers and pinch-faced pinkie-swearers to find Gully at the school gate—snout in effect. He smiled grimly. There was a wet patch on his shorts that he kept trying to cover with his hand.

"What's that?" I asked.

"Someone drew something on me. I washed it off."

"Drew what?"

"A penis." He said it like Sean Connery. *Penish*.

"Who did it?"

He looked away, wrote something in the sky.

"Tell me who it was. I'll sort him out."

He stopped writing to shout, "IT'S OKAY!"

"FINE!" I shouted back.

We walked, our bag straps slapping in sync. Gully started talking about the Bricker. It took me a while to link what he was saying to his memo, and by the time I made the connection, he was in another realm.

"It's entirely possible that the Bricker is an anti-Semite. He also hit Ada's Cakes and Bernard Levon, Tax Accountant."

"But, Gully, we're not Jewish."

"Maybe the Bricker only hit our shop to make it look like he doesn't have a vendetta against the Jewish community."

"The brick was random."

"Nothing is random." Gully stopped walking; he thwacked his snout and drummed the side of his head with the heel of his hand repeatedly until I had to seize his wrist. Beneath the snout he had on what Dad called his "dazey-face." The one where he stood too close and swayed, and his brow loomed like a slab of granite. And if he was silent, it was spooky; but if he talked, all you could see was the pink of his mouth moving, his eyes so earnest it hurt.

"Nancy's coming tonight," I told him, trying to distract.

"Agent Cole, KGB."

"Affirmative."

"Tell her, *The red shoe is in the grass.*"

"I said she's coming—you can tell her yourself."

Gully nodded, but he still didn't move.

"Come on. Friday night fish and chips, remember?"

Seconds passed. And then he smiled as if seized with happiness at the prospect of flake. He adjusted his backpack and walked, carefully avoiding the cracks in the pavement.

Two hours later Nancy and I were sitting on the back counter, swinging our feet and meditating on the Wall of Woe. Dad's "display" had started as a cheap way of concealing rising damp and turned into a mosaic of the world's worst record covers: *Top of the Pops, Hooked on Classics*, the New Seekers, Herb Alpert and the Tijuana Brass, Jimmy Shand's Scottish dance band . . . Some customers laughed, others left. I figured most would rather face rising damp than Barry Gibb and Barbra Streisand in matching white silky pantsuits.

"Barry looks worried," Nancy noted.

"It's his hair, it's too fluffy."

"It could be his jeans. They're sectioning him."

Dad turned to Nancy, his eyebrows knitted like furry summer caterpillars. "Where are you working these days?"

"The Purple Onion," Nancy said. "You know that dome on the foreshore? It's what they call a 'pop-up' bar."

"Is it now?"

"They've used this hideous purple paint and all this brush fencing. It's like being inside a testicle."

Dad opened his mouth and then closed it again. He turned back to his records, shaking his head.

The shop was empty of customers. Gully patrolled the floor, searching for dividers in need of rejuvenation. Dad was playing Hank Williams, which meant he was feeling sorry for himself. He fixed the lady cop's card to the till. I picked it up; the corners were curled.

"Why don't you call her?"

Dad ignored me. He had the pricing gun in his hand and a stack of vinyl piled high on the counter in front of him, but he couldn't seem to connect the two.

"Do you want me to call her?" Nancy suggested.

Dad gave her a pained look.

"I'm really looking forward to this movie." Nancy shot me a wink. She quoted breathily, *"You and I are the same. We do what we do because we have to. Because we don't know any other way."*

I could see Dad's shoulders tense.

Nancy went on blithely. "We have to dress up." And for Dad's benefit. "People dress vintage."

"And what time will it finish?" Dad asked.

Nancy grinned. "Don't worry, I'll get her home before pumpkin time."

Gully piped up. "I wish I could go. I love Jane Crawford."

"*Joan* Crawford," I snapped. "You don't even know who she is!"

Nancy swooped down from the counter to hug Gully. She squished his face. She was the only person he would take this from.

He blushed and stammered, "The—the red shoe is in the grass."

Nancy nodded. "The eagle flies at midnight."

"Don't encourage him," Dad barked. The look on Nancy's face—it was as if he'd slapped her.

"Sorry," she said, standing up and stepping back.

Hank Williams continued to moan.

"What's wrong with him?" Gully wanted to know.

"He's long gone and lonesome," I said. "It's a serious condition." I was eyeing Dad. I couldn't work out if he was in a mood about Nancy or Evil Eve Brennan or what. The clock struck six, and Dad set the pricing gun down. "Who's getting the chips?"

"I'll go." Nancy grabbed a fifty off him and sashayed out the door.

Dad turned to me. "Think we'll ever see her again?"

I kicked him in the back of the knee, hard enough to make a noise but not hard enough to hurt.

A SORT OF SICKNESS

WE WERE STILL WAITING for the chips when Steve Sharp walked in with a man-bag full of vinyl. Steve Sharp was a local "face." Dad knew him from the old days, but only peripherally because Dad was a failed musician, and Steve Sharp was seriously famous. His band, the City Sparrows, cracked the American charts in the mid-nineties. Then came money, fame, excess, tragedy, legal hassles, rehab, and recovery. His third wife, Yayoi Osa-Sharp, was the tragedy. She killed herself, and would have killed their son, Otis, too, if not for the arrival of two Jehovas, who smelled the gas and smashed a window with a miniature temple from the Sharps' ornamental Zen garden. Post-rehab Steve Sharp was a model citizen. He performed for charity, was a Buddhist and celibate. He also happened to be a real estate developer, Dad was fond of pointing out.

As far as regular customers went, the Double S was a good one because he knew his stuff and what he sold in was, if not rare, then at least interesting. Despite this, Dad followed record store code of treating him like dirt. First he ignored him. Then he glared at him. Eventually he cleared some space on the counter and grunted, "All right. What have you got?"

"Treasure." Steve Sharp caught my eye and kept it.

I blushed—just because he was famous, and handsome for an old guy. He pulled his records out and stretched his arms behind his head, eyes back on me. He made me feel see-through. I smiled, but my gums were like thick strips of Blu Tack, and my lips took too long to land.

Dad started the buy, flipping through the stack, separating the good, the bad, and the ugly. He checked the sides, occasionally running his thumb lightly over the grooves, or using his fingernail to check the depth of a scratch. He did this with a poker face.

Steve Sharp drifted over to New Acquisitions. I wondered why he sold records in—he couldn't need the money. But that was the way with most customers. Apart from the occasional death-rock kid trying to flog his grandma's Charles Aznavour LPs, Wishing Well patrons were collectors—buying and selling and abhorring or evangelizing their twelve inches of vinyl shellac. It was a sort of sickness.

"Seventy-five cash, ninety trade," Dad barked.

"What about the Hendrix?"

"It's got a pressing fault."

Steve Sharp looked momentarily dismayed, and then he shrugged, a fluid arch that said whatever happened in the world could never be enough to rattle him. "Trade, then. Put it on my tab."

Gully gripped his stomach. "Where's Nancy?"

Seconds later she sauntered in, all hair and skin and lipstick and tea rose and salt and vinegar. For a moment she met Steve Sharp in the aisle. He moved to the left; Nancy moved to the left. He moved to the right, and the same thing happened. "Sorry." He touched her arm, let her pass, and watched her as she went. Nancy bustled up to the counter. She picked up a stray single, sniffed it, arched an eyebrow. "Smells like teen spirit."

Dad laughed. Steve Sharp laughed too. I felt a squeeze inside. I don't know why it had to hurt, the way she dialed the world with her little finger.

Steve Sharp said, "My son's band's playing at the Paradise. It's sold out, but I've got comps. You girls want to go?"

"Not Sky," Dad said.

Nancy was swinging her legs, eating her chips, blanking everyone beautifully, but I knew her. I knew she was interested.

Dad grunted. "I thought they were pulling the Paradise down."

Steve Sharp smiled. "Tonight's the last night."

"You don't have to look so happy about it."

"It's called progress, Bill."

Dad muttered something under his breath. He filled in the Buys Book with Steve Sharp's details, writing

"FAMOUS" in the space where he was supposed to write his license number. "You want anything today?"

"Nope." Steve took the tickets out of his pocket and put them in Elvis's tray, swapping them for a couple of tapes.

He walked out. After a beat Gully said, "What's called progress?"

Dad grunted again. "It's his company that's doing the wrecking."

TOTAL CATNIP

IN MY BEDROOM NANCY stared at Steve Sharp's tickets like they were made of gold. "Have you seen Otis Sharp? He's, like, total catnip. I'd like to find him down a dark alley." She fanned herself with the tickets. "We're going."

"What about Joan Crawford?"

Nancy turned to look at me reproachfully. "Sky, do you want to be the person doing things, or the person watching other people do things?"

Chastised, I busied myself by the record player. I put on Bobbie Gentry because her voice was warm *and* cool, and even when she sang about bad situations, she somehow made them sound tolerable. Nancy stepped out of her jeans, pulled off her top, and started at my wardrobe.

"What's wrong with your clothes?" I joked.

"What's wrong with your *dad*? Man, when I was your age, I was never home."

"I don't *hate* being at home."

Nancy turned to roll her eyes at me. She pulled a few dresses out and draped them over my bed. She lit a cigarette. I pushed the window open farther. It was still hot outside. Heaving. I took off my school dress, revealing my singlet and undies. I took off my shoes and socks, and the article about Mia Casey fluttered to the floor.

"What's that?" Nancy said, reaching for it.

I watched her face as she read the article; it stayed blank, inscrutable. Then she said soberly, "I hope she was a party girl; I hope she lived before she died."

"Her brother, Lucas? He's *Luke*. The guy Dad's hired."

"Potato guy?" Nancy's eyes widened. "Now you definitely have to go for him. Hot *and* tragic. That's a winning combination."

"I wouldn't know what to do."

Nancy flung her top at me. "Put this on." I did as she told me. The top was tight; it made me look like I had boobs. Nancy nodded. "Good. Wear my jeans. You can be me tonight."

Nancy's jeans were also tight. I had to lie down to do up the zip. Nancy flopped on the bed next to me, topless. Bobbie Gentry was singing about a girl whose mama pimped her out, and I was trying not to look at Nancy's boobs.

"Sky?"

"What?"

She found my hand and placed it on her breast. It felt soft, full. I didn't dare look at her. Then she put her hand on my head and brought it to hers. What followed was the weird putty feeling of her lips mashed against mine.

"Open your mouth," she murmured. I opened my mouth. Nancy's tongue touched mine, a warm shock. I let her kiss me. I kissed her back. I felt like I was underwater. She pulled away. "So you know what to do with Luke Casey," she said.

"Of course," I managed, my face on fire.

Nancy went back to my wardrobe; she decided on a gold top over spandex pants. She fluffed her hair and fixed her makeup, then did mine. When she'd finished my face, I didn't even recognize myself.

Nancy licked her thumb and smudged away some rouge. "There's this festival in Japan called the Atukai Cursing Festival. Men go out in boats, wearing white clothing, and travelers stand along the river and swear at them. Can you imagine? The Japanese are nuts. I'm so going." Nancy paused and then hung her head out the window and shouted, "Fuckkkkkk!"

No one shouted back.

We went downstairs. Gully balked at my makeup. "You look old," he said, peering at me uncertainly.

"Thanks so much."

Dad gulped at my forced cleavage. "Put a coat on." He sounded three beers deep.

"But it's boiling."

"Here." He shoved my denim jacket at me. I shrugged

it on, winching it at my chest. I went to give him a kiss on the cheek, but he'd already turned away. I had been feeling guilty about lying, but now resentment glittered in me. *Fine,* I thought, letting the jacket go slack. *Fuck you too.*

As we walked away from the shop, I tried to still the waves of excitement vibrating through my body. Nancy cut through Acland Street, my mum's spindly peach pumps scoring the night, and I was like the shark with half its brain turned off, following her into the deep.

BARBARIANS

I D." THE BOUNCER'S ARM was like a railway sleeper.

I floundered. Looked at Nancy. She was smiling up at him, trying to win him over, but the guy was made of stone. The line outside the Paradise went right around the block. The crowd was older, late teens, twentysomethings. They were a sea of black with signature items: a cape here, platform boots there. There was crazy hair and conversation-piece piercings, chalk-faced girls with Cleopatra eyes, guys who looked like mad revolutionaries.

We shuffled aside from the bouncer's bored stare, and just at that moment a noise sounded like a gunshot. All heads turned to the road. Nancy seized the moment, grabbing my arm and hauling me under the velvet rope. And then we were inside and trundling up the great staircase. I could smell thrift-shop shirts and orange oil, Red Bull and adrenaline.

Nancy went to the bar, returning with two blue drinks. She herded me to a corner. A cute guy in a trilby hat with a medic's bag and stethoscope wandered over. Nancy whispered something in his ear. He checked her heart and then gave her a small packet. Nancy kissed him hard on the mouth. The guy hung around, looking at me. He spoke loudly in my ear.

"Are you here for FUCKBOMB or Otis?"

"What's the difference?"

"You don't know? Oh, this is good." He pressed his shoulder into mine. His breath smelled like caramels.

"FUCKBOMB have to go first because they thin out the crowd. They're fucking *barbarians*. You ever see those old videos of the Sex Pistols where kids are throttling each other when they dance? Like that. Otis is slick but shady. All the ladies love Otis."

"Okay." I smiled weakly.

He moved in closer. He looked at me like he knew me.

"You're a baby," he said.

"I'm nearly sixteen."

Nancy cut in. "Skylark, pay the guy."

"Huh?"

Trilby moved in for a wet open-mouthed kiss. I took his tongue poking mine for three seconds before breaking away. He doffed his hat. "Enjoy."

I turned to Nancy. "What was that?"

She answered by showing me her palm. A foil square glinted in it. She opened it and I saw tiny rocks.

I hesitated. "What's it going to do?"

"Nothing bad."

"How long will it last?"

"A few hours. Don't worry. It's like floating."

Floating didn't sound so bad. I pushed away thoughts of Dad and Gully. I let her put the rocks on my tongue. The swirling in my stomach sharpened. Soon the lights dimmed and the crowd thickened. Three guys stalked out onto the stage. The singer was only wearing undies and football socks. He was long-faced and ugly, hairy as an Afghan hound.

FUCKBOMB! The audience screamed against a batallion of drums.

FUCKBOMB! Like getting hit across the head with a sheet metal plate, again and again and again.

FUCKBOMB! Two girls in front of me throttle-danced, smiling huge.

Nancy and I thrashed around. The songs were short and violent and thrilling. By the time the band imploded in a squall of feedback, I was sweating and panting. My body hummed like a tuning fork that had just been hit.

"Do you feel it yet?" Nancy whispered.

My face hurt, but whether it was from smiling or clenching, I couldn't tell. The DJ was playing something that sounded like psychotic circus music. Nancy grabbed my wrists.

"Do you feel it now?"

My face would have answered her question, but her eyes were closed.

Later in the ladies' room I clung to a corner and watched the light fall on the beaded curtain. I'd lost

Nancy, and time had become a slippery thing. I had no idea how long I'd been in there, but it felt like forever. The room was jammed with girls checking hair and hurling laughter. A group of them was wearing silver scarves. They looked like a girl gang or a dance troupe. One of them saw me staring and gave me a dirty look. I shifted my focus to the wallpaper. I wanted desperately to straighten up, but the patterns on the wallpaper were moving. I turned my face to the wall, aware that I looked weird, unable to do anything about it. I went inside myself. And when I came back out, I heard voices volleying. A door slammed. The towel dispenser jammed. Somebody yelled, "He's starting!"

THE GIRLFRIENDS OF OTIS

THE CROWD HAD CHANGED. All of the color had moved up to the front. The girls with silver scarves hugged the lip of the stage and swayed like tendrils. I counted seven of them. Seven girls in silver scarves. The lights dimmed again. The audience *aah*ed. The curtains parted and a big screen showed slides of abandoned barns, plane wrecks, clouds. The band wandered out wearing animal masks and started up some moody swirl of noise. Otis—the fox—took his mask off. He was in a sharkskin suit and had a silver scarf, same as the girls. The thought hit: *the Girlfriends of Otis.* I remembered Nancy then and cast around for her, but the images on the screen tumbled down and I felt as though I was tumbling with them.

Otis emitted a series of sobs into his microphone. He had hair like bracken and skin like space dust. His songs were spells that floated up and weaved around the chandeliers and then were swallowed by the crowd. When he smiled, it was like his face fragmented and I didn't know where to look. It was merge music—there were no sharp edges; it was all meandering and liquid.

After a long time he lifted his hand and the band stopped. The audience seemed to be holding its breath. Otis's speaking voice was higher than I'd expected. It didn't completely break the spell, but it woke me up a little.

"It's the end of an era," he piped. "The Paradise's coming down. Take a piece before you go."

I saw Nancy then. She was on the edge of the stage, half-hidden by the curtain. Her face was flushed and dreamy—almost unrecognizable.

One by one the band members ambled off the stage until it was only Otis left with the hum of the amplifiers. Then: Crash. Shudder. Blink. It was over.

Otis lingered talking to various scarf girls. Nancy inched forward and picked up his fox head. She looked weird standing there, cradling it and staring at him with an expression that wasn't far from Gully's dazeyface. Then Otis was talking closely to her. He put his arm around her shoulders. I could hear the scarf girls seething. It was like a hive, the noise.

I called out to Nancy. She saw me, but she didn't move. I climbed onto the stage, but even when I was standing next to her, she felt far away.

"Hey." I tugged her sleeve.

"Hey." Her eyes stayed on Otis. He turned to talk to someone else, and then Nancy was fumbling in her pocket, trying to give me something. Money.

"For the taxi," she said.

Otis was moving, and she followed after him, somehow wormed her way back under his arm.

I held the note dumbly and watched as they glided to the exit. Nancy's eyes were straight; her mouth hid her smile. The scarf girls formed two lines to make a kind of bower. They waved their scarves, and if one or two hit Nancy full in the face, she didn't seem fazed.

Then someone grabbed the song list. Someone else tore down a poster. All around me people were stealing their pieces of the Paradise. I went back to the ladies' room, where a girl was fashioning lengths of the beaded curtain into necklaces. It was Quinn Bishop. She recognized me and raised her eyebrows. "Sky*lark*. Do your parents know you're here?"

And just like that, I started crying. It was weird. Embarrassing. The tears kept coming.

Quinn watched me cry. She placed an awkward hand on my shoulder. And then she looped a bead necklace over my head. I splashed water on my face and looked at my reflection in the mirror. I didn't look startled anymore. I looked wretched.

Quinn squeezed my shoulder. "What are you on?"

"My friend gave me something."

"Good friend?"

I nodded, wiping my eyes.

"You going home? You want to walk with me?"

I was so grateful I had to stop myself from blubbering all over again.

As we walked out of the theater, all I could think of was wreck and plunder. As well as the beads around her neck, Quinn had an SLR camera. She took my picture. Then she snapped the emptying street, the passing cars.

"So you're into Otis?"

"Yeah," I said. "He's like . . . total catnip."

Quinn laughed. She looked completely different from in school. Open, friendly. Less bulldog-ish. She paused to snap two guys who'd scaled the sides of the building to lift letters from the marquee. Old Eli Wallace was in his camp chair, watching, his face an etching of despair. Quinn snapped him, too. Finally she lowered the camera. She pointed city-side. "I'm that way."

I pointed in the other direction. "I'm that way."

"I know," she said. "The record shop, right?"

We smiled at each other like we shared a secret and then forked off.

DESPERATE ANIMALS

I WENT FROM GLOOM to rushing. I felt jittery, alive. I half ran, half skipped with one hand on my new necklace, my heart pounding. The night was all things coming together and breaking apart, like kaleidoscope patterns, like kisses. The lights of McDonald's pulsed. The traffic was a steady throb. The clown face of Luna Park looked sinister in the half dark. I slipped onto the park path, into shadows, and heard movement by the iron siding, a scraping noise. Behind the bushes someone was pasting up a poster—a poster of Mia Casey.

"Hey!" My voice broke the quiet. The guy turned around, startled, and he was Luke.

"It's you," I said, but that was all I could manage before lights swamped us and a voice commanded: "Stay where you are."

Luke pushed past me, knocking me down. In that moment I heard something fall. I crouched and my fingers found Luke's glasses. I clutched them and stood up again, and blinked into the torch of a big-faced policeman. There was another officer with him. She stepped out of the shadows, and I saw she was Constable Eve Brennan. My mind whirled on the smallness of St. Kilda and the bigness of my fuck-up.

"You're Bill's kid, right?"

I nodded.

"What are you doing?"

I found my voice. "Going home."

"Who was with you?"

"I don't know. I don't know him."

"Where have you been?"

I opened my mouth, but nothing came out.

Eve exchanged a weary look with her partner. "Come on."

The police car smelled like warm leatherette and antiseptic. I was in the backseat but not cuffed or anything. I pictured the cell, bread and water, skeleton keys. I played out scenarios—the stuff of Gully's dreams: being printed and interrogated under a bare, swinging bulb. The station loomed, all matte black and windows. Eve's eyes met mine in her mirror. She gave me a firm smile. "I'll take you home."

I nodded. She was giving me something and I was grateful. I hoped I didn't look stoned, or that if I did, Dad would be too pissed to notice.

Eve came up with me. Up our skinny stairs into the too-bright light of the living room, where Dad was dozing in front of an old movie. She clocked the empties but didn't mention them. When Dad saw her, his face was like the picture for HAPPY on Gully's chart. When he saw me, it changed to CONFUSED, and then ANGRY.

"Where the hell have you been?"

I still had Luke's glasses in my hand. I moved them behind my back. "The movie finished early, so we went to a party. It's okay. I'm okay. Nothing happened."

Dad ran his hand through his hair and then brought it down quickly to cover his beer belly. He was in his friendlies: a Cosmic Psychos T-shirt and football shorts that showed way too much leg. I looked at our flat the way Eve would see it: the unwashed dishes, the Pee-wee Herman poster, the bills skewered on the antlers Mum had found at a garage sale a lifetime ago.

"She was walking home by herself," Eve reported.

Dad stared at me. "Where's Nancy?"

I smiled a stupid involuntary smile, and Dad's face just crumpled.

"Are you drunk?"

I ran then, out of the room and up the stairs, heading off the next wave of tears. I locked my door and took off Nancy's top and pressed my face into it. It smelled of her. My whole room still had the air of her, of promise and adventure. I wished I'd never left it. My record player was still turning, playing nothing, the belt squealing faintly with each revolution like a tiny, desperate animal. I stood close to it and watched it spinning around and around. And then I turned it off and went to bed.

In my dream Mia Casey and I were sitting on St. Kilda Pier, our toes just touching the surface of the water. We were eating icy poles and talking about the future.

Mia said, "I want to work with kids. Like, maybe I'll do face painting."

"I'm going to work in the shop," I told her. "Forever."

Nancy was there. She was sitting nearby, but she wouldn't look at us. She hung her head, and her hair was a curtain. I could see her face reflected on the water, but it appeared dark and distorted.

"Sky," Mia said. "The water's really fucking cold."

She jumped then and I couldn't see her after that. It was as if she'd never been there. No ripples formed. The water stayed flat, silver and shiny as a coin.

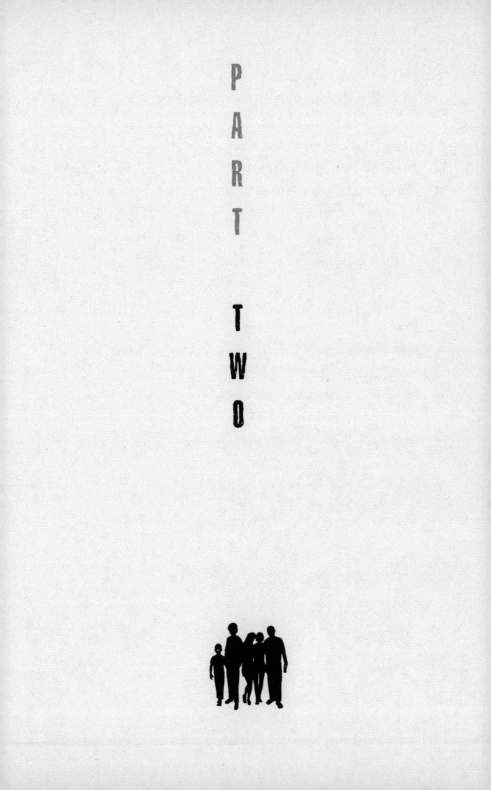

PART TWO

A LEVEL OF DISCOMFORT

THE MIND IS A funny thing. It takes all those images that rush you every second of every day and mixes them up with your memories until you can't remember what's yours and what's complete fiction. When I woke up on Saturday morning with a desert mouth and a disco head, the first thing I thought of was Mia Casey. On the floor by my bed lay the following:

> —*Nancy's clothes*
> —*the bead necklace from the Paradise*
> —*the article about Mia Casey*
> —*Luke Casey's glasses*

I picked up the article and stared at it. "What happened to you?" I asked her image.

I'm trying to tell you, her eyes replied.

I pressed the page against my forehead and closed my eyes again. My head felt drum-tight. I lay still for a long time, listening to the cars and the birds and my breathing. I tried to sort the jumble of images crashing through my mind: chandeliers, cocktails, clouds, scarf girls. I relived Quinn's small kindness, Luke and Mia in the park in the dark. My bottom lip felt sore. I touched it and thought about the drug dealer kissing me, walking me backward into the wall. *Whoosh!* My stomach felt like a lift that had just dropped two floors. I almost enjoyed the feeling, but then I flashed on Nancy going off with Otis. Her groupie glaze, the way she'd given me taxi money as if it could make up for deserting me. But then, I reasoned, Nancy wasn't used to looking after someone. Just because I did it for Gully didn't mean other people had to do it for me.

I lifted the window and inhaled the warm air, then climbed out of bed and started to put things in order. I folded Nancy's clothes. I put Mia back in my wallet and the bead necklace around my neck. I didn't know what to do with Luke's glasses. I tried them on, smiling at my blurred reflection. He was only a little bit blind.

There was a knock on my door.

"Sky, Sky, Sky."

"Gully, Gully, Gully." I let him in. He was in full snout and tool belt, carrying a tray of tea and toast.

"Dad said you were sick. So I made you this."

"Thanks." I crunched into the toast while Gully studied me.

"Why are your eyes all black?"

"It's makeup."

Gully was standing very straight. His eyes darted

about. He let out a groaning noise, fiddled with his snout, and then spoke from behind his hand in a clipped staccato.

"I have intel."

"What?"

"I woke up in the middle of the night and I was hearing funny noises, so I went downstairs. . . ."

I hurried him along by waving my hand.

"And I saw Dad and the police officer. Remember Constable Eve Brennan? They were . . ." He stopped and blinked forcefully. "Wrestling, I think."

"Just wipe it from your mind," I suggested.

Gully nodded. Then: "The new operative is downstairs."

"Huh?"

"Luke Casey."

My stomach dipped. I tried to keep a straight face, blowing coolly on my tea. "What's he like?"

"Tall. Doesn't say much. He smokes Peter Stuyvesants and carries a sketchbook. He has a muscular twitch." Gully brought a finger to his cheek. "Here. Indicates a level of discomfort."

"Good," I said. "We wouldn't want him to be too comfortable."

Gully *chh*ed his fist. Then he relaxed his pose, jiggling his shoulders. He could never stay completely still. "Come down? It's too different."

"Um. Half a tick."

I was not interested in Luke Casey. I was not going to jump him or fall for his hot and tragic combo. I told myself this as I changed out of my pj's into the green dress that Nancy said made me look like an ingenue. I went to the bathroom and washed my face. My hair was cowlicky. No amount of wet would suppress the bumps. At the last minute I remembered Luke's glasses and put them in my bag.

"How are you going to play it?" Nancy had asked. "I say, do it on the down-low, act like you don't even see him." But that was before last night.

I stood on the pavement looking through the shop window. Dad and Luke were behind the counter, their heads bent together like dark, punk flowers. They had similar angular frames and unkempt hair. I took Luke's glasses out of my bag and put them on. I didn't smile or move my head. I just stood there, bespectacled. It was the kind of move that Nancy would pull. I was slightly proud of myself until I realized he was short-sighted and probably couldn't see me. Then I took his glasses off and entered the shop as nonchalantly as my speedy heart would allow. As I walked toward him, I was thinking this: Nancy was right, Luke was pretty. I considered his cheekbones, the soft set of his mouth, and suddenly it was like I was standing in front of him, waiting to be remembered.

DON'T ENGAGE

AD WAS PLAYING LOVE'S *Da Capo*, which meant he was in a good mood despite my infraction. He was moony, lovestruck even. He waited until "Orange Skies" had floated off on little pop clouds before paying me any attention.

"How's your head?"

"How's yours?"

Dad ignored that and made the introductions. "Skylark, this is Luke. Luke, Skylark."

Luke had been sitting on my stool. He stood and offered his hand. He had paint around his fingernails, a mist of black that looked gangrenous. We shook hands. I looked into his eyes and saw that he recognized me. He didn't smile; he swallowed. *He's nervous,* I thought. And that made me nervous. When I brought my hand back, it felt limp and like it didn't belong to me. The rest of me was messy too. My stomach felt like it had slipped its moorings.

Dad was in impressive-boss mode. "Now that you've decided to grace us with your presence, I have to see a man about some records. I'll take Gully."

I felt panic snapping at me. I might have even clutched Dad's arm. "Wait"—I lowered my voice— "You're going to leave us alone?"

Dad looked from me to Luke. "You'll be fine," he said. "Give Luke the grand tour."

"How long are you going to be?"

"Not long."

Dad shuffled off with Gully in tow. I slipped onto his stool. Then it was me and Luke sitting side by side while sweet psychedelic pop sparkled around us. I took Luke's glasses out of my pocket and put them on the counter. He waited for a few seconds, then put them on. "Thanks," he said, not looking at me.

"Don't mention it." Side one ended and then it was so silent that I could hear the migration of dust motes.

It was a typical Saturday. St. Kilda throbbed, but the Wishing Well was as sedate as a gentleman caller. The sun slanted in the window, highlighting acne pits, shiny pates, and dandruff. Wishing Well customers were mostly old and male and nerdy. They could tell you why Paul McCartney was barefoot on the cover of *Abbey Road*, but they couldn't manage basic hygiene. I wondered if Luke had noticed the smell yet. Memories and mildew.

"So," I started, "the grand tour."

Luke sat up and took his sketchbook from his pocket. He flipped to a clean page, primed a black fine-liner. His props were like Gully's; they made me soften toward him. I tried to toughen up again.

"Have you ever worked in a record shop?"

"I worked in a pub," he offered.

"That's good. That means you're used to crazies."

"You get crazies here?"

"Oh yeah."

"What kind of crazies?"

"Like you might get a customer trying to explain how the alignment of the stars affected the recording process of Rick Wakeman's *The Six Wives of Henry the Eighth*. . . . Dad's rule is this: don't engage."

"That's a good rule."

I pointed to the till. "This is the till, for the purposes of storing money. Behind there is the record file for dupes and raries." I pulled out five copies of Paul Mauriat's *Blooming Hits*. "Dupes." Then a near-mint *On the Beach*. "Rarey."

Luke nodded. "Dupes and raries."

I pointed to the medieval ledger chained to the counter. "This is the Buys Book for the purposes of buying. When someone sells something in, we write it down. We have to take ID in case it turns out to be stolen."

I flicked back through the pages. It was all in there: the decline and fall. Looking at the Buys Book depressed me. It was already starting to resemble a relic.

"We used to buy a lot more, but these days most people put their records online."

"But not your dad," Luke noted.

"He's analog. He's like a caveman. No CDs. Don't even think about downloads. He's even scared of karaoke."

"Fair enough," Luke said. "Karaoke's pretty terrifying."

I laughed, surprised at the joke. Luke smiled properly. It was a shock to see his face break like that. His eyes crinkled, his cheeks bunched, his lips went tight across good, straight teeth. He looked beautiful. For a second I lost my way, and then I found it again. I showed him the stockroom. I showed him the loo. I showed him where the kettle was. I told him I liked my tea black and Dad only drank his when it was cold, and then I sat down and pretended to read *Record Collector*.

Luke stayed standing. After a while he cleared his throat.

I looked up.

"Is there something I should be doing?" he asked.

"There's some Windex back there. You can clean the cabinets."

I watched Luke work from behind the cover. His brow went smooth as he wiped the glass, but he never really relaxed his shoulders. If I stood over by the window, I could see an edge of Mia on the wall. I wanted to ask Luke about her, but there was no way to do that without appearing interested, and I wasn't quite ready to admit to that. I grabbed some records from the Going Out pile and spent the next half hour fattening the racks. I had this feeling that if I didn't move, I might start talking, and if I started talking, I wouldn't be able to control what came out: *I dreamed about your sister. I feel like we were friends. Ray said she was a party girl, but Ray's full of shit.* Every time I caught myself trying to sneak a look at Luke, I reminded myself of his interloper status. Yes, he was pretty, but he was in my space.

Luke looked up. His eyes met mine and he smiled again. This time it was brief and there was something tender-awkward in it. I couldn't work out what it reminded me of, but then I realized it was Mia. I saw her walking with her bare feet and flower crown— the image almost felt religious. What had it been like, to lose her? Were they close? Had Mia looked out for Luke the way I looked out for Gully? Where was she buried? What song had they played at her funeral? All my unanswered questions were banking up, making my brain hurt. I turned up the volume and let drums and cymbals and driving guitars numb my mind.

Dad and Gully returned just before lunch. They came with toasties and tales of grade-three records—g-sale stock, an insult to the discerning musicologist.

"How's it been?" Dad asked.

Luke and I gave him matching blank faces.

"Why so quiet?" Gully demanded. It was only then that I realized there was no music playing. The last record had finished half an hour ago, and I'd been too distracted to notice. It was a shop rule that we took turns playing records. Dad was a hog. Gully would get stuck on the same track forever. Now Dad turned to Luke like Mr. Magnanimous.

"Put something on. Whatever you like."

To some eyes this could look like a test. The first track a newbie played might set the tone for his employment. Luke was right to look uncertain. He wandered around the aisles for ages, coming back with Simon & Garfunkel.

I snorted. Even Gully shook his head.

"What?" Luke asked.

"That record doesn't tell me anything about your inner emotional landscape," I told him.

Luke stayed poker-faced. "Don't have one of those."

"Bullshit."

"Sky—don't psychoanalyze the new guy." Dad turned to Luke. "Gully reads faces, Skylark reads records. We, the Martins, have superpowers."

"What's yours?" Luke said.

"Dad's able to drink a whole case in a single sitting," I cracked. The look on Dad's face made me wish that I hadn't. Actually, *that* was his superpower: Dad was great at guilting me. Simon & Garfunkel's harmonies folded over each other. My brain was squeezing into itself.

Luke's presence put a bump in things. Dad wouldn't stop talking, booming his rock alphabet from Aswad to the Zombies. Gully was infected too, more boisterous than usual, with groaning and fidgeting at a premium.

He crowded Luke, putting his snout up close. "Who do you like?"

Luke blinked. "What do you mean?"

"I mean, what are you into? We're Team Lennon, Team Richards. Dad likes punk and country. He thinks Arthur Lee is underrated and Bono should be shot. Sky likes sixties psych and folk. I'm into space music."

"I don't think he understands you, Gully," I said.

"Skylark," Dad warned.

"I like a bit of everything," Luke said.

I scoffed again. "People who say they like everything have no taste. And having no taste is worse than having bad taste." Dad was giving me the evil eye, but I kept going. "I know you. You don't care about history or culture or lineage. If Lonnie Donegan had never made a skiffle, then the Beatles would never have happened, and if the Beatles and Bob Dylan had never gotten stoned together, then John Lennon would never have written 'Norwegian Wood,' and if Joni Mitchell hadn't mesmerized half the Byrds, then all those LA singer-songwriters wouldn't have bared their souls and gotten all mellow and flaccid and then morphed into stadium rockers like the Eagles and Fleetwood Mac, and then punk rock would never have happened, and then . . ."

Luke's mouth twitched. He was laughing at me. I turned away, my cheeks hot. It wasn't even my rant; it was Dad's. I heard Luke's voice behind me.

"You don't know me," he said.

I walked out then. It was four-ish. The sun was climbing and the shoppers were rampant. I felt stupid and hungover. My throat all thick. I clomped along and didn't stop until I was standing on the little gray bridge looking down at the Purple Onion in all its brush-fenced testicular glory.

SOFT-BOILED

ANCY WAS A LOUSY waitress. She couldn't hide her boredom. She stood with her pen poised over her notebook and stared past the customers' faces. Even with her mouth all twisted she looked beautiful: her hair piled on top of her head, a big silk rose pinned to one side; red lipstick. Nancy's apron was longer than her shorts. Her skin looked like something you could sleep on. I hung around the spider grass feeling inferior for a while and then moseyed down to the sandbags that skirted the dome. Nancy grinned when she saw me. She urged me over and hollered to no one, "Taking a break!" And then we were arranging ourselves on the milk crates outside, our faces turned to the sea.

"Dollbaby, I'm dying! Do you know how hard it is to be polite to those fuckers? I feel like I'm in one of those boxes they used to lock hysterical women in back before they invented Valium."

"You don't look hysterical." I stopped short. Nancy was wearing a silver scarf, same as the girls from Otis's gig. She had it tied like a neckerchief. I couldn't stop staring at it.

"What?" she asked.

"Nothing," I said. Then: "Where did you go? You just left me there. Anything could have happened."

Nancy was unmoved. "And did it?"

"Did what?"

"Did anything happen?"

I told her how I'd seen Luke Casey pasting up the picture of Mia, and how I'd gone home in a cop car and Dad was pissed off but yet to hand down his punishment. Nancy nodded, a small smile playing on her lips.

"Dollbaby, I don't know. You say you want to go to the zoo, and then you get upset when the monkeys throw shit on you." She used her cigarette like a pointer. "You had an adventure."

"I did, didn't I?" I said in surprise.

"I knew you'd be okay." Nancy cracked her neck. She looked proud and tough. In the pulp fiction novel of our life Nancy was a doll, a dame, a dizzy broad. But I was soft-boiled. I watched everything from a distance with my knuckles wedged between my teeth.

"What else?" she asked.

I told her about Luke Casey in the shop, on my stool, looking hot, but wholly uneducated in the area of popular music.

"He might be sucking up to Dad," I added.

"Let me tell you how to handle Luke Casey," Nancy said. She had a copy of *Neon* open and was systematically burning holes through random hipsters on the "Seen/Scene" page with her cigarette.

"Tell your dad he's frotting you."

"What's frotting?"

"Rubbing up against you."

"There's a word for that?"

"It's French. The French have a word for everything." Nancy tossed her hair and rearranged her scarf, and that was when I saw the clutch of plum-dark lovebites. She saw me looking.

"Did you have an adventure?" I asked.

Nancy's lips were pressed tight. Then she turned to me and her eyes were shining. "Okay," she gushed. "I'm in love. I'm, like, annihilated. He's not like anyone I've met before. You saw him, right?"

"I saw him."

"So after the Paradise he takes me to this penthouse, and it has three-hundred-sixty-degree views and everything in there is, like, new. I was scared to sit down."

I couldn't imagine Nancy being scared of anything.

"He had his friend with him. The fat guitarist. Rocky. He had a girl too."

"Sounds cozy. What did you do?"

Nancy sighed. "Everything."

I forced a smile and waited for the story. Nancy's stories were like the little films I played myself when no one was watching. But for once she wasn't telling.

We sat in silence, me with my smile, she with her secret, while the tide rolled in and tourists took photographs of each other posing with the sea and the city behind them. I was jealous. Of him, of her and him. And I couldn't think of anything to say. The day had gone flat. Seagulls wheeled in the sky. Behind us traffic undulated, a steady hum. I could see steamer ships and the smudge of the western suburbs across the water.

"So are you going to see him again?"

"Of course."

"When?"

"I don't know. Soon."

"What about us?" I blurted.

"We can still hang out. You can meet him. Maybe you and Rocky—"

"I'm not doing anything with anyone called Rocky."

I stared at the hole-eyed hipsters and the tin full of sand and lipsticky cigarette butts. And then I changed the subject, pointing across the water.

"I lived in Newport once, for about a month. My grandparents live there. Mum's parents. We don't see them anymore. Dad took us there after Mum left. They had labels all over the house. Light switch here, that kind of thing. Also heaps of tinned food. Dad said it was because they lived through the Second World War.

"My great-grandpa lost his nose in the war," Nancy said. "His whole nose, clean off." A frown marred her face, and she drummed her foot into the dead grass.

"Is he still around?" I asked. It was the first time Nancy had ever said anything about family.

She shook her head, staring dully.

"What about your mum and dad?"

Nancy moved her mouth around. "They were arse-holes. End of. I'd better get back in."

"It's my birthday next week," I reminded her. Then it was my turn to scuff the grass. "Dad probably won't let me out of the house."

"Do you want me to talk to him?"

"You'd do that?"

"Sure." She shrugged. "We're friends, aren't we?" Nancy leaned into me. "Hey—do I smell?"

I sniffed. Her hair smelled musky.

"I came straight here. I didn't even shower."

"Gross."

Nancy grinned and pinched my cheek. I felt a seize inside. This idea that Nancy was getting further and further away. But she jumped up with renewed energy. She kissed both my cheeks and then went back for a third. And once again I felt a rush, a hum, a thrill.

I walked home confused. What was wrong with me? Was I crushing on Nancy or crushing on Luke? I was like a dog with its tongue flopping out, ready to give everything to the first person who patted me. I had to protect myself. I couldn't keep going with all my nerves on the surface of my skin.

Luke was out on the street having a cigarette. He

had one foot back against the plane tree and a dreamy look on his face. I didn't acknowledge him, just stuck my head in the door and announced to Dad that I needed to lie down.

"I want to talk to you," he said, wagging his finger.

"Later."

Up in my room I put on Kraftwerk's "Neon Lights" and flopped onto my bed. The song was so long and glittery-sad, it made me feel like I was falling off the face of the earth. I pushed my face into my pillow and slept straight through till morning. If I had any dreams, I didn't remember them.

FIGHTIN' WORDS

SKYLARK, YOU'RE GROUNDED."

"I'm grounded?"

"Yes. School, shop, home. That's it."

"I hate to break it to you, but those three things, that's pretty much all I do."

"Don't be smart, it doesn't suit you."

"You're crap at this, Dad."

He sighed. "I know."

It was Sunday morning. We were in the kitchen, surrounded by a mess presided over by two empty Dunlops bottles.

Dad smelled pickled. His eyes were rheumy. I stared at his tear troughs, the flecks of gray in his beard.

"Alcohol is very aging," I reported. "Alcohol and sugar."

"I'm not worried about my age," Dad said. "I'm worried about yours. You're only fifteen—"

"I'll be sixteen next week."

"You're only fifteen and Nancy's . . . older."

"But she's pretty immature." I was angling for a smile. It worked. Dad's eyes crinkled almost to extinction.

"Don't," he said. "I'm serious. I didn't know where you were. And then you come in with Eve and you looked all . . ." He waved his hand around. "You can't be walking home alone like that. That's the worst of it. This isn't the country. Bad things happen to girls out there."

"I know," I said, thinking of Mia, and then suddenly I was talking about her, putting her on the table.

"Did you know about Luke's sister?"

Dad looked wary. "How do you know about that?"

"I worked it out."

"Don't tell Gully."

"I won't."

"Jesus, imagine what he'd do with that. We'd never hear the end of it."

"I said I won't tell him."

"And don't go talking to Luke about it."

"Why not?"

"Because she's dead, that's why not. Don't be an idiot, Sky."

I pondered this. "He might want to talk about her. Not everyone is as closed up as you are."

"Closed up! Who's closed up?"

"You are. Vesna said it. She said you were like those Chinese boxes that no one can figure out how to open."

"Vesna said that?"

Dad was smiling fondly—maybe an image of Vesna

in her Daisy Dukes was scrolling across his mind. Vesna had been his pub-friend-turned-girlfriend. She'd moved in for a little while after Mum vamoosed, and tried to sort us all out. Vesna was addicted to Zumba and beauty products. She watched infomercials with religious zeal. She had this facelift device that she used to wear strapped to her cheeks while she did the dishes. It made her look like an anglerfish. When she moved out, Vesna bequeathed us her Fitball. For a long time it migrated from room to room, and no one ever went near it. I was sure this was symbolic.

Dad was looking misty; I tried to get his attention back. "Nancy calls you Bill the Patriarch. She thinks you're looking for a surrogate son."

"Nancy's wrong."

"She says you want someone to pass your knowledge on to, and you won't pass it on to me because I have a vagina."

Dad spluttered coffee across the kitchen table. He shook his head and pointed at me.

"You're grounded."

"What about my birthday? School break, Christmas?"

Dad kept shaking his head. "And I want you to look after Gully. The shop's getting busier—you should keep him occupied."

"With what?"

Half of Dad's mouth turned upward. "Help him solve the Bricker case."

"I thought we weren't supposed to encourage him."
I folded my arms on the table and rested my chin on
my wristbone. All the talk had made me tired. Maybe
I hadn't quite recovered from Friday night; maybe I
never would recover. Suddenly I felt weepy. My voice
cracked a little. "Why can't we just hang around the
shop? Last holidays—"

"That was different."

"I'll say." I picked up the Dunlops bottles and
clanged them into the recycling bin. Last summer—
post-rehab—all Gully and I did was hang around the
shop. We played at buying, and Dad spent long hours
lying on the back-room floor listening to Can on his
oversize headphones. I didn't want to look at Dad now,
so I looked around the kitchen instead. Why was it
always so messy? The sink was piled with dishes; the
day had hardly started, and already an army of ants
was trekking over crumbs and jam blobs. My eyes took
in evidence of Eve—brown lipstick on a coffee mug, a
long red hair atop the bits-and-stuff bowl.

Above our heads the toilet flushed.

Dad lowered his voice. "Grounded. Gully. Boom.
That's it."

He stood up, pushed his chair back. I flinched at the
scraping and glared at his retreating back. Then I sank
my forehead onto my arms. I flashed on Nancy again.
The French had a word for everything: even for that
thing you wished you'd said. *L'esprit de l'escalier.* The

wit of the staircase. What I wished I'd said was this: *You can't have been that worried about me Friday night because when Eve brought me home, you were dozing with a reef of empties at your feet and after I went to bed, the pair of you—I don't even want to know.* But I couldn't have said that. It was too big. Those were fightin' words, and no one had my back.

BLACK HEAT

THE MARKET AGAIN: THE coffee, the toasties, the boys with bolt earrings and girls in frayed cut-offs, the tourists clapping for koalas, for cupcakes, for white dreadlocked guys playing didgeridoos, the hubbub and hum, and the Martin family looking for all the world like we'd wandered onto the wrong film set and any moment some short guy with a megaphone was going to move us along.

I was acting normal enough, but inside I was freaking. It was because of the Paradise, the gig. Now that I had some distance from it, I couldn't stop thinking about it. It was like the line between Before and After. A door had opened. As long as I kept thinking about it, the door would stay open. If it shut, I'd be back to my boring self. Through the opera glasses I studied the faces of passersby, looking for black-clad kids, night people. Maybe I was looking for myself.

Dad nicked the glasses, pitched his head at an awkward angle.

"Who are you looking for?" I asked.

"Eve said she might come down."

Gully gave me the big eyes and turned to Dad. "Are you going to wrestle again?"

Dad's face flamed behind the glasses. I couldn't hide the smirk from my voice.

"You should be thanking me for bringing you together. If I hadn't gone out, she wouldn't have picked me up. . . ."

Dad's look said I should let it lie, but I was feeling defiant. How come Dad got to wrestle a lady cop while I got grounded? What was that all about? And something else rankled. I considered the ways Dad had messed up. He could be a crank and a slipping-down drunk, but Gully and I weathered it and never put any demands on him.

"It's not fair," I said hotly.

"Skylark."

Gully blinked, his snout twitching. "What's not fair?"

"Nothing," Dad and I chorused.

Gully's eyes bounced between us. Then he checked his watch, *chh*ed his fist, and got into character.

"Date: Sunday, December seventh. Time: 0950 hours. Location: O'Donnell Gardens. Preparing for House Meeting. Rolling."

"Item: Christmas. I want night vision goggles. And Baked Alaska. For Christmas lunch everyone gets to bring someone." He appealed to Dad. "You bring Eve. . . ."

Dad tried to look cool, but his soft grin gave him away.

Gully turned to me. "Agent Sky. Will you ask Agent Cole, KGB?"

I made a noncommittal noise. I couldn't imagine Nancy at Christmas lunch. I couldn't imagine her doing ordinary things. She had no family, she had no past. It was as if she'd arrived in St. Kilda fully formed like something out of a myth—flaming hair and gladiator sandals—Nancy—*Nana*—she could leave anytime with no consideration for my feelings.

I checked Ray's through the opera glasses. He was in situ; but there was no sign of Nancy.

Gully: "Item: It has come to my attention that *someone* is putting the remote in a variety of places. It should be kept on the coffee table At. All. Times."

"Roger that." Dad elbowed me, trying to jostle a smile. He cut in, mimicking Gully. "Item: When does school break start?"

"Not next week but the week after," I droned.

"What will I *do* with you two?"

"There's always buying lessons. . . ."

"There's more to life than the shop, Skylark."

"I know that." I looked at him. His tone was a tell. "How's the shop doing, anyway?"

"You leave me to worry about that."

"You think Boy Wonder's going to bring you luck?"

"Don't be catty—it doesn't suit you."

"I like Luke Casey," Gully declared. "He's stout."

"How do you know?" I was surprised. Gully never liked the new recruits.

"I looked in his sketchbook. I analyzed his handwriting. He's stout. Trustworthy. I can tell." Gully put his hand on Dad's shoulder and fixed him with his superdetective's you-will-cooperate stare. "Is Agent Luke working today?"

"*Agent* Luke!" I snorted in mild disgust.

"I'm going to profile him." Gully flexed his fingers and snapped his snout back into place.

"This should be fun," Dad murmured. He was trying to catch my eye, but I wouldn't give him the satisfaction.

A beardy, bug-eyed customer stopped at Dad's feet and forced an elaborate fist bump.

"Bill, my man."

"Hey, Ed, what gives?" Dad asked mildly.

"They're paving paradise, baby." The man shone his rubbery smile on our blank faces. "She's coming down. I'll save you a seat."

Dad, Gully, and I hesitated for a stark second, then scrambled to our feet.

Down on the Lower Esplanade cranes moved like metal dinosaurs. We, the Martin family, milled on the fringe of protestors. Eli Wallace was still in his chair, still with the sign. Gully jumped to ask him about the

Bricker—did he remember seeing a white Jeep doing the rounds?—but Eli couldn't comprehend, and then came the first of a series of crashes that stunned the crowd and stilled the air. The machines made quick work. The landscape looked all wrong—too much sky and too much sea. Forty-eight hours ago I'd been inside. The Paradise had been alive then; now it was rubble. Dad looked a little green. He said, "A hundred years she's been standing and she's down in half an hour."

"That's it." Eli stared straight ahead, smacking his lips as if he had a bad taste in his mouth. Around us the protestors shifted and murmured their dissent.

A car cruised beyond the cordoned-off area, a white Mercedes, old, license plate ZAZEN. Steve Sharp stepped out. The passenger door opened and Otis joined him. He was looking casual enough in his jeans and flip-flops, but his sunglasses were Gucci. He stood listless as his father talked to a guy in a hard hat.

"Bastard!" a protestor shouted.

Louder voices followed:

"Pig!"

"Scumbag!"

Eli Wallace had a bag of oranges by his side. He took one out and hurled it at Steve Sharp. He was a great shot. More and more hands reached in, and then Steve Sharp was getting pelted. Otis, too. The ex–rock star's son looked feeble. He looked like he was about to cry. And then he was crying. My first reaction was to laugh because here was this guy, this *god* in Nancy's eyes, and he was falling apart from a few pieces of fruit. But then something in Otis's expression reminded me of Gully, and after that I couldn't laugh. Steve Sharp shielded Otis from the barrage. He bundled him back into his car and then drove off, stone-faced. I glimpsed Otis in the passenger seat, head buried in his hands.

Gully was confused and a little bit delighted at the happenings. He wanted to throw an orange too, but the target had gone and hard-hat guy was heading over with his fists clenched. As we scarpered, Eli Wallace was crowing. "What are you gonna do—hit an old man?"

"Dad, why were they throwing oranges at Steve Sharp?" Gully asked.

"Because he's greedy. His company's called Urban Renewal. They buy up the old properties and turn them into apartments. You can't do that without pissing off a few people. You know he's bought the yoga center. He wants the whole corner. We're the last man standing. He doesn't think about where people have to go."

I remembered the forgotten flyer on the counter. "If you're so upset about it, why didn't you go to the protest?"

Dad frowned. "Because sometimes you have to accept the inevitable."

I stopped walking. "Dad, that's so depressing." I

watched him open the shop with his head lowered. Even Gully looked thoughtful as he followed him in.

Dad played Nick Cave for old time's sake, closing his eyes because his life, too, was like a river all sucked into the ground. I thought about the Paradise, and what could happen to the space where a place used to be—the ghosts of gigs past. Maybe Dad was thinking about that too. He was quieter than usual. After a while I stopped thinking about the Paradise and started thinking about Luke Casey. I pretended I wasn't waiting for him. And when he rolled in, damp hair and soap shine and an almost smile, I pretended I wasn't remotely interested. I said, "Hi" like, whatever, and moved away. I put records out; I sorted stock; I sat on the back counter and read *Record Collector*. Dad walked Luke through Cleaning Vinyl 101. Gully hovered in case his expertise—or entertainment—was required. I tried to maintain a hard edge, but I was weak. Intermittently, Luke looked at me and intermittently I let him.

That night, I stayed up late listening to records and sorting my box of beautiful people. I tried not to feel pathetic as I did this. I smoothed out my Nancy doll and teamed her up with a hot guy who could have been Otis if his hair was longer. I found a Luke-a-like with soft hair and spectacles and a pixie-faced starlet who could have been me if I succumbed to surgery. I took the picture of Mia out of my wallet and invited her to the party, moving us around into different configurations. We were a gang of great friends. We laughed at each other's jokes. We knew each other's secrets. We were young and hot, and no grandstanding grown-ups were going to tell us what to do.

At one a.m. I went up to the roof. I sunk homebrew and peered over the palm trees and clouds and shingles. The sky was infinite and starry, and I felt like I was in a movie. I played Them doing "Gloria." The world was all black heat and a badass riff. Nancy's stories roiled inside my head: bikers and club kids and vampires and red lipstick and visible tan lines and five-o'clock shadows and surprise couplings on fire exits.

Out there Luke was pasting up pictures of his sister, and bad things were happening to young girls.

Out there there were no rules, and Nancy was doing more than I could dream of.

Memo from Agent Seagull Martin

Profile: Luke Casey
New Operative, Bill's Wishing Well—
Effective December 6
Date: Sunday, December 7
Agent: Seagull Martin

The subject says he doesn't know his
height, but I would pick him at six
feet. He is Caucasian, has dark hair
that could use a cut, and wears square,
black-rimmed glasses. A casual dresser,
he was born and educated in Adelaide,
the city of churches and serial killers.
When he was little, he wanted to be a
firefighter. His worst memory of primary
school is being forced to fight a kid he
knew he couldn't beat. He couldn't ask
his dad about fighting because his dad
is a minister and doesn't believe in
violence, so he would sneak into movies
in Chinatown to study chops. But when
he tried to use said chops on the kid, he
found they didn't work, and he ended
up with a shiner so big, he had to look
at everything sideways. He is in favor

of *Monkey*. In high school the subject
enjoyed art and English. He has been
studying graphic design, but he decided
he wanted to do something radical and
so came here. He wears a size-thirteen
shoe and a leather wristband. He is
a smoker and does not believe in the
afterlife. He is scared of heights and
seaweed. When I asked him what his
greatest regret was, he looked blank—
and refused to answer. His favorite food
is sausages and mash, but he won't
eat kidneys. He suffers from insomnia,
wears SPF 30 every day. He likes St.
Kilda because the sky seems bigger
here. Says he looks at the sky and
imagines it as a hemisphere floating
in some unrecognizable space, encased
in a bubble. His best spy trait is that
he works well alone. His role model is
Steve McQueen in *The Great Escape*. He
has no plans for Christmas.

ACTION
Recommend we invite the subject to
Christmas lunch.

RECON #1: COUNCIL OFFICES

THERE'S THIS EPISODE OF *The Twilight Zone* that never failed to remind me of Gully. It's about a six-year-old boy with godlike powers. He can read minds and control the weather, and if he doesn't like someone, he simply wishes them away to a mysterious cornfield. Everyone is scared of him—even his parents—they're careful to tell him only good things, but in the end the community cracks under pressure. I'm not saying Dad and I were scared of Gully—he didn't have magic powers—but he didn't hear "no" very often.

Monday after school he was waiting at the gate with his snout on, drinking coffee as all real detectives do. When he saw me, he hiked his eyebrows and chucked the dregs, tough-guy style, before placing his mug gently on the grass. He *chh*ed his fist and gave me the specs. "Date: Monday, December eighth. Time: 1535 hours. Location: Mercer High School front entrance. Operation Council Jeep Discovery preparing now."

I started laughing. Sometimes Gully was good value—and it had been a dull, dull day. I'd been preparing for Quinn, making assumptions. I'd even worn the bead necklace, which earned me more than the usual weird looks. At lunchtime I was at the library computer, ready, but she never showed. I didn't expect her absence to make me feel so hollow.

The afternoon was neon-bright. Gully swing-walked and issued directives.

"As per my memo, we go to the council and get the names of all the people who have registered white Jeeps in St. Kilda."

"Gully, there's no way they'll tell you."

"Oh yeah? What if I show them . . . this?" He flashed a detective badge. It was paper, painstakingly traced. Just looking at it made my hand cramp.

"Come on!" he yelled.

A feeling came over me—something like surrendering the remote control. I thought of Dad. I would follow Gully on all his ridiculous schemes. This was my penance.

And so we trooped on down to the town hall. We took a number and planted ourselves on the plaid chairs for forty minutes. I didn't even try to convince Gully to take his mask off. When we were called, he lurched into the booth, his eyes like flints, his snout close to making contact. The anemic-looking clerk couldn't hide his irritation. He was lucky there was a pane of plexiglass between us.

"You want me to give you the addresses of people

with white Jeeps registered in the Port Phillip ordinance? Impossible. There are privacy laws."

Gully rocked back and forth. He flicked his snout with his little finger and wrote something in the sky. "So, is it classified information?"

"It is," the clerk replied with a sarcastic smile.

Gully wavered. He didn't seem to know what to do next. I imagined in his mind this was as far as his fantasy went, this asking of the question. He skywrote a little faster and started to hum. The clerk was getting crabby and that made me crabby. That made me want to stand there until sundown. And then I saw Ray, rolling in with files in hand. His work clothes made him look like an extra from a 1970s documentary about white-collar criminals. He had flapped his tie over his shoulder, and one of his shirt buttons was missing; white orca flesh glinted underneath.

I banged my palm on the glass. "RAY!"

The crabby clerk rose from his chair. "Excuse *me*!"

Ray shambled over, pacified the clerk. He appeared baffled by Gully's snout; I guess it was seeing us out of context, but then he clicked his fingers.

"Nancy's friend, right?"

"Sky. Hey, can you help us?"

Gully got to ask his question all over again. Ray wheezed and listened. His forehead was sweaty. He patted it with a handkerchief. Then he winked.

"You kids go wait for me out front."

I parked on the stone steps and stared out at the street. Gully was flapping like crazy and making groaning noises, competing with the peak-hour traffic.

Ray surfaced, a blobby mirage. He pulled a rolled-up piece of paper from his slacks. Gully wanted it but looked well aware that the paper had been nestled near Ray's tackle. Curiosity won. He grasped for it, but Ray held on. "Tell no one."

Gully nodded solemnly.

Ray couldn't be serious. He had to be messing with us. As if he would risk his job for a boy in a pig snout. But then he turned to me and his eyes were greedy. He took my hand in his clammy meat hook.

"Does Nancy talk about me?" He pressed my hand and let out a little puffing sigh. "What I mean is, does she like me?"

I felt slightly sick, and I also felt like laughing. I managed to hold it in. I looked him in the eye. "Sure. She likes you."

Ray dropped my hand and hugged himself. Another button threatened to pop. "She's got that classic beauty. Like Rita Hayworth." His face shifted, a subtle tell I couldn't decipher. Gully would have known what it meant, but Gully had taken his intel behind a tree and was reading it covertly.

"Do you know where she is?" Ray asked.

"I saw her Saturday."

"You're doing better than me, then."

He puffed again. Looked back at the glass door. But he didn't leave. He took some gum out of his pocket and offered me a stick. I shook my head. And then it was like I'd caught Gully's disease. The question came out. Boom. Like that.

"How did you know Mia Casey?"

It would have been better if Ray had looked taken aback. I didn't believe his sorrowful expression or his answer. "A fallen robin. I only met her in passing."

I wanted to ask him about the party girl thing. Instead this came out: "How long has Nancy lived with you?"

Ray's eyes searched the sky. "Five months?"

"She ever tell you where she's from?"

"I never asked. This is St. Kilda. Everyone's from somewhere else."

"I'm not."

Ray laughed. "Honey, you're from another time."

I looked down at my school dress and the palms of my hands. I wanted a fast retort, but I wasn't even sure if he was insulting me.

"Etymology," Ray said, propping his finger like a professor. "There's another St. Kilda in the Hebrides. You can only get there by boat. It's uninhabited now, but people lived there right up until the late 1800s. They spoke old Norse mixed with Gaelic, and lived off vegetables and traded the oil from the seabirds that gathered on their crazy rocks. But they were doomed. Ask me why."

"Why?" I asked dutifully.

"The Industrial Age killed them. They were murdered by progress. The last St. Kildans had to be evacuated. A handful came to Melbourne and found their way here . . . at least that's what they say." Ray smiled. "To be a true St. Kildan, you have to admit to isolation, to weirdness, to loser-dom."

Seconds and trams and cars passed. The world was turning on a spit, and I still couldn't tell if Ray was insulting me.

"Well," I said. "Thanks for helping my brother."

"You can pay me back in sexual favors."

"I'm fifteen, Ray."

He pinched my shoulder. "You girls are so touchy."

LUKE ON FAST-FORWARD

ULLY AND I REACHED the shop just after five. Luke had already left, and Drago had dropped off the CCTV unit. It wasn't quite the high-tech security camera of Gully's dreams, but he was still excited. He speed-read the manual and made the Weird Sisters pretend to steal something so he could see how it looked. Dad had set up a screener out in the back. I sat with Gully for a preview. The camera swapped between shop and street view: we saw the plane tree, occasional cars, then customers doing the usual wander around the blue haze, picking noses, dropping food. When I came back out, Dad winked at me, because I was moody and he was trying to cheer me up, and because when Gully was firing on all cylinders, he could be brilliant or a complete shit and in this case it was the former.

"What do you think of the new technology?" he said.

"I think Gully's going to get square eyes."

As I said it, an idea sparked.

That night I was the one staying late in the shop. I rewound the tape to the start and watched Luke Casey on fast-forward. The video camera was old, but it had an impressive zoom function. I could see Luke up close, his default half smile, those eyes with lashes sooty as a soft toy's. I watched him arrive and have a cup of tea. I watched him listening to Dad, patiently, for hours. He was overly solicitous with the customers. He looked them in the eye and gave them smiles and paper sacks. Sometimes he'd stop and stare at a far-off point. I fancied he was looking at the poster of Mia. Luke went out for a cigarette at eleven, one, and three. He drank four cups of tea. His muscular twitch was on the wane, but in its place were new tells. He had a habit of brushing his hair back from his eyes if Dad was going on for too long, and he worried that leather wristband all the time except when he took it off to clean vinyl.

I knew what I was doing was creepy. I told myself I was assessing Luke critically, as a favor for Dad, a productivity review. Luke really wasn't record shop material. He held records like they were frisbees. When he cleaned vinyl, his cloth was too damp, so he left streaks. I watched him work and I stockpiled his fails, and during a lull I texted Nancy.

Guess who I'm watching on CCTV?

Miraculously, she texted back. *Who?*

Luke Casey!

Seconds later my phone rang.

"Perve!" Nancy brayed. "How's he looking?"

"Tragi-hot."

"What else?" Nancy's voice sounded faraway, like she was talking in a cave.

"I saw Ray today. He asked about you."

"I'm in the shit because I haven't been home."

"Why should he care?"

"Because he's pissy, and he can't boil an egg."

"So where are you?"

Nancy laughed low, sounding like Vesna. "What else?"

"Ray asked me if you liked him. I said yes."

"Gag. Thanks a lot."

"He's seriously creepy, Nancy."

"I know." She sighed. "He wants me to go to this party. He's bought a dress for me and everything. I'm supposed to make him look good."

"Are you going?"

"Depends. Why—you're not worried about me, are you?"

"Hardly." I scoffed, then chewed on the silence. I had a feeling that the gap between what we said and what we actually wanted to say was getting wider and wider.

The phone crackled.

"Where are you?" I asked again.

The phone cut off. I waited for Nancy to call back; she didn't. I plummeted into a funk. I saw Nancy moving through the magic doors at the airport. I imagined her boarding the plane, creating her own turbulence, while I was left with a five-dollar coffee in the airport lounge. To cheer myself up, I watched a little more Luke. Rewinding and fast-forwarding. The sameness of his actions was somehow comforting. And then something happened. For a period he was alone behind the counter. I saw him look around and then take a cassette tape out of his jacket pocket. He put it in the player, pressed play, and waited. It took him a while to work out that the button was set to phono. Finally he figured that out, and the spindles must have been turning then. He sat back on the stool, took his sketchbook out and started drawing. His hand moved loose and so fast I almost couldn't see the pen. As he listened and sketched, his forehead crinkled. When a customer approached, Luke covered his sketchbook. He ejected the tape and repocketed it. He served the customer— smiling—but even after he'd gone, Luke's face never made it back to the calm of Before.

What was he listening to? What was he sketching? Why did he have to wait until he was alone?

These questions rang, and I sat for a long time sparking and bristling and wondering if this was what a crush felt like. Was it real or manufactured? Nancy had put the suggestion there, right from the get-go. What if she'd never said "Yours"? Would I have even thought it? It wasn't the first time I'd had a guy at close proximity—school was full of them. But those guys were creeps; their eyes weren't steady the way Luke's were. Their skin was too spotty, their eyes too slippery, and their knees tapped their desk lids with some desperate rhythm I didn't want to catch.

I gave up. I was hungry. The later I stayed, the more work I would have to pretend to have done. I put a fresh tape in for the morning, hit record, and went back into the shop. Luke had left his wristband on the counter. I scooped it up. Later in my room I laced it around my wrist. I snapped the button and closed my eyes and imagined that his pulse was still on it and merging with mine.

Memo #2

Memo from Agent Seagull Martin to Agent
Skylark Martin
Date: Monday, December 8
Agent: Seagull Martin
Address: 34 Blessington St., St. Kilda, upstairs

POINT THE FIRST:
I now have names and addresses of all
registered Jeep owners in the Port Phillip
ordinance. There are eleven names in total.

POINT THE SECOND:
According to Asif Patel, proprietor, 7-Eleven,
the two women egged the same week as the
Bricker's reign of devastation were "prossies."

POINT THE THIRD:
CCTV acquired—should the white Jeep pass
at night, we may get a make on the plates, Bob
willing, even the driver.

ACTION
Investigate addresses of registered Jeep
owners—ongoing.
Interview prossies.

RECON #2: VALE AND GREEVES

MONDAY BECAME TUESDAY BECAME Wednesday. Quinn Bishop was still a no-show. I amused myself by Googling Otis Sharp. The computer spat up the same two images. The first was a snap of the family Sharp: Steve and Yayoi and baby Otis at the foot of Mount Fuji. Even as a baby, Otis looked regal. The second image was of rock star Otis in his snakeskin suit and silver scarf; girls flopped on the floor around him like so many dead fish. I stared at the picture for ages. It didn't gel with the image of Otis in the back of his dad's car. It made me think of Mum. How she presented one way, but behind it she was someone else. I called up her website and wrote in the Ask Me Anything box: *How does it feel to be such a fake?*

Gully stepped up investigations. We went through Ray's list, staking out various flats and houses for the express purpose of gathering intel on Jeep owners. From Asif's blurry 7-Eleven CCTV photograph, we knew the Jeep had a couple of bumper stickers, but so far nothing we'd seen correlated. Gully used a Polaroid to photograph each Jeep. He performed the age-old spy tactic of nick-knocking and, where possible, also photographed whoever answered their door. He made copious nonsensical notes and pilfered mail from the owners' letterboxes. In Gully's mind he was above the law, and I didn't have the energy to correct him.

"Date: Wednesday, December tenth. Time: 1617 hours. Location: St. Kilda, corner of Vale and Greeves streets. Operation Prossies in effect. *Chh!*" Gully lowered his fist and peered left and right. Confusion furrowed his brow.

"Where are the prossies?"

I smacked his arm lightly. He reacted as if I'd tried to electrocute him.

"Stop calling them that," I said. "Say 'working girls.'"

"Why?"

"Because it sounds better."

"Why?"

I stopped. There was a stone in my shoe.

"I don't know, Gully."

The red light area was not the wilderness of discarded condoms and push-up bras I'd imagined. Instead it looked positively family. Old workers' terraces nestled against modern townhouses. I saw prayer flags, droopy camellias, kids' bikes. I lifted my bead necklace to the sun and watched the rays bounce around.

"What now?" I grouched.

"Now we wait." Gully began his exercises, a mangled kind of tai chi. He pushed his bum out and windmilled his arms and closed his eyes and aimed his snout to the sky. Five minutes passed with no cars.

I drummed my foot. "This is dumb. Let's go."

But just as I spoke, a car turned in and stopped. A girl jumped out of the passenger seat. She was tall and thin with nimbus hair. She propped against a wall and poked around her purse. Gully strode toward her and it dawned on me: he's actually going to interrogate her. Suddenly this seemed like the worst idea in the world. I lunged to stop him, catching his sleeve and tearing it. I could tell by his face that any interference would result in a shit fit, but I couldn't seem to stop myself from trying to stop him.

"Don't," I started.

"It's okay!" Gully shrieked, shaking me off, plowing forward.

A hundred public meltdowns flashed through my mind. I used to be able to get him in a pretzel hold, but he was bigger now. The best I could manage was to grip his arm, and shield my face from his free one.

We struggled. It felt like forever, but it was only a few seconds. Then Gully bit my arm.

"Ouch!" I cried, letting go of him. "Fucking hell!"

"Mouth!" Gully snapped, then quickly, with his head down, said, "Sorry."

I rubbed my arm. The skin was already swelling. "Look!" I said, shoving it into his eyeline. "Those're your teeth marks."

"Well, you shouldn't have tried to strangle me." Gully rejigged his snout; he took a breath and released a small ninja cry. I backed off, wincing as he faced the girl and fired questions like popgun pellets.

"Were you working the week of November twenty-second? Did you get egged? Two girls got egged right here. Were they friends of yours? Do you know about it? Did you happen to see a white Jeep?"

The girl considered Gully: his ripped shirt, his skewed snout, his hair sticking up all staticky.

He blustered under her gaze. "I'm a detective and this is important. *Chh!*"

She gave me a terse smile. "Off his meds?"

I bit my lip. I wanted to cry. It was so hot and my head hurt and Gully was impossible. Maybe the girl could tell I was on the brink. She held up her hand.

"Try the collective. Streetwise, Inkerman Street. Ask for Granny." She pointed at Gully. "Watch your temper, little man." Then she flicked her hair and walked away.

UGLY MUGS

STREETWISE HAD A SHOPFRONT, but they weren't selling anything. The windows were lined with photographs of men under a sign that said, UGLY MUGS, NAME AND SHAME. Gully and I paused before each picture. The men were a mix of ages; some looked hard and some looked stupid and some had regret rounding their brows. Most seemed to have been snapped on the fly. Below each image was text detailing crimes and misdemeanors. I read the comments—there was nothing savory. I wanted to shield Gully's eyes, but he read without flinching. He may have been small and weird, but in a way Gully was more comfortable with the world than I was. He was never shocked. He sought for the rational explanation and if it didn't exist, he was perfectly happy to invent it.

A ponytailed woman in a halter top sat at a desk, facing a computer. From the door she looked young, but as we got closer, I saw her dragon skin. Her face was so creased it looked like a relief map. Her eyes grazed me, Gully, Gully's snout.

"Are you Granny?" Gully sounded so imperious.

The woman had a voice like Velcro. "I might be. Who are you?"

He took his notebook out. "Agent Detective Seagull Martin, Special Investigations Unit." He cleared his throat. "Two, uh, working girls were egged the week of November twenty-second. I'm after information."

Granny pushed back on her rolly chair. She folded her arms in front of her considerable chest. Gully was searching her face but coming up short. He said, "Our dad owns the record shop on Blessington Street. Our window was bricked November twenty-seventh. I have a hunch that the two cases are connected."

"You have a hunch." Granny's eyes met mine. There was a light in hers that made me feel less anxious. "Is he a vigilante?"

"Something like that."

"I don't mind a vigilante if he's on the right side." Granny rose slowly. She had a turgid, waltzing walk. As she moved farther away from us, I could see that her foot was encased in a plaster boot.

"I got shot," she said, not looking back. "You know how many bones there are in the foot? A fuckload. Pardon my French. Phalanges, metatarsals, sesamoids—shattered."

She edged behind a partition.

Gully was brimming. He gave me the two thumbs-up.

"We're close," he whispered.

I shook my head—it was too soon to call the mission a success.

On the pinboard above Granny's desk I clocked a photo of Johnny Depp in his *Pirates of the Caribbean* gear with a sign that read, "Happy 70th, you scurvy wench!" Also: a certificate of appreciation from St. Kilda Primary School. Also: six photos of the same dog—a Jack Russell—modeling a series of knitted vests.

We could hear her gravelly voice from behind the partition. Laughing ruefully, waiting, saying, "I know, I know." Granny re-emerged, taking longer on the way back. Gully was on tiptoes and tenterhooks.

"Cleo says the eggs were thrown from a white Jeep, four young guys, unknowns. No plates, but there were stickers on the back window." She checked her Post-it. "One of them said, LOVE LIVE LOCAL."

"'LOVE LIVE LOCAL'?" Gully repeated.

"That's what she said."

Gully wrote the words in bold capitals. He remembered to say thank you. He looked like he was fit to combust. I hooked my arm around his shoulders. For once he let me.

"Come on," I said.

The Ugly Mugs were inside as well. Granny saw me staring.

"Curb crawlers," she said. "Head cases. Give the girls a hard time. They don't have any protection out there. Rotten eggs are the least of their worries. You got a nice home? A mum and a dad?"

"That's personal information," Gully snapped.

"Gully," I scolded him, then answered Granny with a nod.

Her lips met to form a thin line. "Well, you're lucky."

Out on the street Gully was in full dazey-face.

"White Jeep, four unknowns, LOVE LIVE LOCAL . . . What can it mean?"

"I don't know."

"I'll do a poll—canvas customers."

I was only half listening because something had occurred to me.

"Wait here," I said, ducking back into the building.

"Something else?" Granny asked.

"I wanted to ask if you knew someone."

"That's personal information." She cracked a smile.

I took out my wallet, the photo of Mia.

"She's the one who drowned," Granny said. "But that's all I know about her."

Gully tapped on the window, mugging. When I turned back to Granny, she wasn't smiling. Her voice gave me a chill. "If you go turning rocks over, don't be surprised if you find something slimy."

Her words reverberated all the way back to the shop.

THE WHOLE VINYL EXPERIENCE

LUKE WAS ALONE BEHIND the counter. He was sketching something, biting his lip in concentration while some head-wrecking drone swirled in the air. He flushed when he saw us and squirreled the sketchbook into the pocket of his jacket that was strewn across the stool. He looked up, a little guilty.

"Hi!" I beamed, then regretted it. It was because he looked familiar there, but this was only because I'd watched him on the CCTV. Suddenly I felt like he knew. My heart beat hard and fast, rattling my ribcage.

"Where's Agent Bill?" Gully asked.

"He went out." Luke touched his temple as if to nudge the intel out. "He said Eve's coming for dinner. He needs you to close up and clean up."

"Roger that." Gully did a swift 360 and headed for the door.

"Where are you going?" I hollered at his back.

"I have work to do!" Gully yelled.

Luke flexed and then folded his hands as if they were in the way somehow. He didn't look at me. We had an hour until close. We worked silently in tandem.

He cleaned records, and I graded and organized them according to condition. At one point his elbow brushed mine and I felt a spark. In my mind it grew into a forest fire. I wanted to close my eyes and indulge it, let the branches crackle and pop. Luke was inches away from me. I could see the worn patches on his knees, his hand circling the vinyl. The bright record light was supposed to pick up flaws, but it worked the other way on Luke. He had fine hairs on his arm; the light made them golden. I thought of beaches, salt spray, warm dunes.

He went outside for a smoke. I stared straight ahead, but my hand was creeping across to his stool, his jacket pocket. My fingers felt the spiral binding of his notebook. Quickly, I pulled it out and flipped it open on the stool. My hands felt clumsy; I couldn't turn the pages. I felt like I was reading his soul. There were more pictures than words, street scenes, St. Kilda, and then faces, details of faces. I saw Mia, and then I saw myself. In Luke's sketch I was sitting on the back counter and my eyes were narrowed, a speech bubble said: "Having no taste is worse than having bad taste." Instinct made me look up. Luke was putting out his cigarette, running his hands through his hair. I shoved his sketchbook back into his pocket and rubbed my hands fast on my thighs. Luke came back in and I tried not to look transformed, but I was. This was the thing: Luke had drawn me pretty.

He was back on the stool next to me; his hand was

pale resting on his thigh. I couldn't stop staring at it. It still had paint on it. His fingernails were all raggedy. I looked at his hand and thought about holding it.

Customers came and went. There was nothing I wanted to say to Luke that could pass for casual conversation. After twenty minutes with barely a word between us, Luke turned to me. He looked me right in the eye, and there was the hint of a smile playing on his lips.

He said, "Your dad's weird and your brother's intense."

I laughed a little. "Gully has social problems."

"What's with the mask?"

"He thinks people can read his facial expressions. You ever heard of the Facial Active Coding System?"

Luke shook his head.

"You will."

Luke put his arm up to scratch the back of his neck. I could see the muscles under his skin. Again, I felt like touching him. I imagined I was the kind of girl who could do that.

"Sky?" It was the first time I'd heard him say my name. "I get the feeling you don't want me here."

"It's not personal. Besides, I think I'm changing my mind."

Luke smiled down at the record he was cleaning. And I couldn't stop myself from smiling too. What we had here was a ziplock moment of certainty, of like and like. Outside, shoppers shopped and schoolkids idled, but Luke and I were in one of those bubbles he'd talked about in Gully's profile.

The door burst open, and the Fugg rolled in with his signature scent of beer and sun-dried urine. Even in the heat the Fugg still wore his fur. Under it was a frayed St. Kilda jumper and football shorts. He had scabs on his legs. Also food in his beard, but at least that meant he'd eaten. Most people meeting the Fugg at close range flinched. Not Luke. He jerked his head dude-ishly. "Can I help you?"

I reached behind the counter for the Fugg's stash bag.

"We keep Ernst's stuff here."

I hefted it over. The Fugg picked through, settled on a record, and carried it off to the listening booth/tardis.

Luke and I watched him, the silence between us like a moat. I decided Luke was either shy or disinclined. How hard could a conversation be? But then I couldn't seem to start one either.

"Cool phone booth," Luke said. And I was so grateful, that I couldn't stop the babble flow. I told him how Dad had found the tardis in the *Trading Post* for a hundred dollars and retrofitted it with a stool and record player and headphones. I told him that most record shops limited their listening facilities so you could only hear what they wanted you to hear, but Dad thought that was against the Whole Vinyl Experience. I told him how the Fugg stayed in there for hours and after he left, we had to use air freshener.

"I've seen him on the street," Luke said. "And at the park."

"He's a poet."

I stared at the Fugg through the glass. "I like watching people's faces when they listen to music. I like how it's private. Even at a gig if you're all hearing the same thing, you're really all hearing something different."

Luke didn't say anything for a moment, just watched the Fugg. Then he half turned toward me. My hair had fallen across my eyes, and he moved a finger to lift it. "You do that too. I mean, your face changes."

He stopped suddenly and looked away, but I had a warm feeling growing inside, spreading from toe to tip.

The Fugg came out, his cheeks damp with tears. He put the record back in his bag. He stared at Luke and rumpled and unrumpled his mouth. He bent his creaky body to bow low and when he came back up, he said, "I'm sorry for your loss." And he shuffled off out into the fading sunlight.

Luke sat as if stunned. His face was like a mask. The telltale muscle pulsed on his cheek.

"I know about your sister," I blurted. "It must have been terrible. If anything happened to Gully, I . . . Dad said I wasn't supposed to talk to you about it, but it's hard because I keep thinking about it. I'm sorry. I know that's weird."

Luke was silent.

I bit my lip. "The posters . . . You must miss her."

Still nothing. Seconds passed like exam hours. I didn't know what to say. I'd done exactly what Dad had warned me about, and now Mia was in the shop with us and the feeling of her was growing with every second. I thought about my dreams, and what Ray had said, and even Granny saying the thing about turning over stones.

"I feel like I knew her," I said.

Luke's eyes were like carnival glass; they changed color depending where the light hit. First they were blue and swimmy with sadness, and in the next second they had clouded over.

He looked at me blankly. "You didn't know her. I didn't even know her." He stood then and shrugged his jacket on. "I have to go," he said without looking at me. When he closed the door, it felt like he'd taken all the air out with him.

MATCHING MOHAWKS

BILL THE PATRIARCH WAS no monk. He'd had girlfriends since Mum, but apart from Vesna they'd been mostly doggerel. We'd seen a lot of stonewash over the years. Every so often one of his ladies would come into the Wishing Well feigning interest in, say, an Allman Brothers album. When this happened, Dad would hide out in the back until the coast was clear.

It was different with Eve. Dad was nervous. Drinking nervous. He looked like he'd stopped for a few after the chicken shop. His eyes were shiny, his gait was clumsy, and he was boom-talking all over the place.

"Dad," I said. "Take it easy. Have a glass of water."

He chugged one and then breathed into his cupped hands to determine whether or not his breath smelled. He rushed up to brush his teeth for the third time in twenty minutes.

Eve looked pretty out of uniform. She wore tight jeans and a red cowboy shirt, her hair curled nicely. I liked the way her eyes crinkled when she smiled; and the way her front two teeth crooked into each other, like they were having a conversation. Eve must have seen Dad was tipsy, but she didn't comment on it. She drank too, but I noticed she had water between wines, and she didn't touch the Dunlops. She was easy with me and Gully. And she'd brought some photos of Dad we'd never seen before.

"Dad, why are you all dressed up funny?" Gully asked.

"I'm not dressed up. That's just what I wore back then."

"How'd you get your hair to stay up like that?"

"I used to use honey," Eve answered. "Creamed honey."

I turned the photos over in my hand. The last picture was of Dad and Eve in psychobilly threads with matching Mohawks. Dad's arm was slung around Eve's shoulder. His head was turned. Eve was looking directly at the camera. The expression on her face was almost demure—it looked odd against what they were wearing, how they presented.

"So did you guys go out, or what?" I asked.

Eve looked at Dad. "Not reeeeeallly. I mean, we were all friends then. There was a gang of us who used to hang out."

"I had a crush on you," Dad admitted. He had his elbow on the table, his palm cupping his chin, his expression dreamy.

"Eve used to walk up to straights in the street and

force them into conversation. She could talk about the cricket, or how to get red wine out of white plush-pile. She could talk about the Dow, whatever the bloody Dow is . . ."

Dad was talking to me and Gully, but his eyes were on Eve and then it was like they were in their own bubble and there was nothing we could do to pop it.

Eve said, "Did you hear about the Berlin Bar reunion party?"

Dad nodded. "They sent me an invite. Are you going?"

Eve gave a tiny shrug. "I'm not working."

"You should go together!" I said, clapping my hands.

Dad eyeballed me—he had his finger near his throat, indicating I should cut it out—but I was having too much fun.

He busied himself with his glass and mumbled, "Maybe. I mean, would you want to go?"

It was like watching a couple of teenagers.

Eve teased, "Are you going to dance?"

"If they play Iggy." Dad held his glass like a microphone and growled into it, *"I am the passenger . . ."*

Gully and I groaned and laughed. With the lights soft and everyone's faces all shiny-happy, I felt flooded with warmth—it was like we'd been infected with a buzzing, shaggy loveliness that I guessed meant the best kind of family. Eve tidied our plates. She did it so fast I barely noticed, and then she was filling the sink and boiling the kettle. "Sky, have you got a coffeepot?" She didn't look at Dad as she said this, but I could tell she was trying to sober him up, keep him sweet.

I found the coffeepot. Under cover of dishes' clatter I felt the need to explain, "Dad's nervous."

Eve just smiled and touched my arm. "I know, honey."

After ice cream Gully pulled his notebook out. "Agent Eve? Can I ask you some questions for my profile?"

Her mouth twitched. "Go for it."

"Why did they call you Evil Eve?"

"It was just a nickname. People thought it was funny."

"I don't think it's funny. I don't think you're evil."

I poked his shoulder. "It's not supposed to be literal, Gully."

"I still don't like it." His mouth crooked under his snout. "Why did you become a police officer?"

"I got headhunted. I was in Queensland, doing community work and teaching martial arts to women and children, and someone made me an offer."

"What's your greatest regret?"

Was I imagining it, or did she look at Dad? She laughed to cover it up. "Where do you get these questions?"

Gully tweaked his snout. "That's classified information."

"Agent Gully."

"Yes, Agent Eve."

"Can I ask you something? We had a call from an elderly resident on Robe Street reporting, ah, stalker-like activity from a youth in a pig mask. Know anything about that?"

"It was probably from my stakeout."

"Right. Why Robe Street?"

"Just following a lead," Gully said. "It's okay."

"Actually, it's not." Eve looked at Dad for backup, but he was beery and streets behind the conversation.

"Just don't do it," Dad said. "Whatever it is."

"Well, I will," Gully retorted. "I have to."

He flapped his hand, wrote something in the air, and then proceeded to work his way under the table in small slips. Once he was well under, I said to Eve, "He'll be there for a while now."

"Sorry—I didn't mean to —"

"It's not your fault," Dad said roughly. He aimed his voice under the table. "Someone's just being a bit of a sook."

Gully responded by biting Dad's leg. While Dad sucked his teeth, Gully slunk and cowered.

"Come out," Dad hissed. "This minute."

"NO!" Gully's voice had gone up an octave.

I could see Dad trying to keep it together in front of Eve. He eyeballed me again and I felt my shoulders tighten. I could hear Gully's breathing coming fast and hard. I waited until it slowed and then crouched down. I didn't try to touch him or meet his eye. "Agent Gully," I whispered. "Evacuate!" He nodded sharply and then backed out and away to the safety of the living room.

Don't say anything, I mouthed to Dad, and he nodded and put his hands together in a silent thank-you. It made me feel peevish. I pictured myself shaking my head, saying, *This is what happens when you bring a new person into the mix.* But the trouble with that was I *liked* Eve. I figured she was worth some minor regressions, as long as that was all they were.

I sat with Gully through *Monkey Swallows the Universe.* In the episode, two crazed cannibals called Golden Horn and Silver Horn were on a rampage, eating the souls of holy men to steal their power. They captured Monkey, made him a miniature, and put him in a magic bottle. Things looked dire for a while, but with the help of Pigsy et al, Monkey managed to escape and annihilate the deadly duo. The TV was a balm, and soon enough Gully was all smiles again. We went on to the next episode as the smell of coffee and the sounds of laughter wafted across from the kitchen. I was amazed that Eve could move Dad on from the bottle. Maybe that was her superpower.

"What do you think?" I whispered to Gully.

"I like her," he whispered back. "She has moxie."

Halfway through the episode the picture turned to

snow; then it went black and then we were looking at Mum pre–Galaxy Strobe. She had filmed herself—she must have been experimenting. Her face came close and went far-away. She stood back and belted out a song; then baby Gully wandered past crying, and the last thing we saw was Mum rolling her eyes. I jumped up and turned the TV off. Gully's face was reflected on the black screen. Under the snout his mouth turned down. A few seconds crawled by.

Then:

"What was she like?" He used to ask this all the time. It was sort of a game between us, but now when Gully asked, his voice had an edge to it.

"You know," I said.

"I don't remember. Give me the specs."

"Let's see . . . she never smiled in photos; she always paused before speaking, as if she was talking to a TV audience and not just the guy from the fruit shop; and she used to reapply her lipstick every hour on the hour—"

"Enemy Red by Max Factor." Gully sighed so deep I could feel it in my vertebrae. He pushed his snout back up and showed me his face. "Will we ever see her again?"

I ruffled his hair. "Sure. In dreams. On YouTube."

He nodded. He looked like a little old man. Like Dad put through a way-back machine, minus the beard and black jeans and Residents T-shirt.

More laughter from the kitchen brought us back to Eve and Dad.

Gully wrote something in the air. He said, "Do you think Dad's in love?"

"He's definitely excited."

"Constable Eve Brennan is exciting," Gully affirmed. Then he yawned and pushed his snout into sleeping state, loose around his neck.

We crashed on the couch. I woke up just as Eve was leaving. It was *late* late. I could hear Eve and Dad making their way down the stairs, sounding merry. I padded over to the window and peeked out from the curtain. I saw Dad open Eve's car door for her, and then they merged into a kiss. I watched them, holding my breath, then creeped back to the couch. When Dad came back, I pretended to be asleep. I heard him open the fridge. I heard the twist top of beer. He put on an Al Green record and crooned along. Dad was hopeless. He was so happy he had to have a drink. For a few seconds I was annoyed with him, and then I fell back to sleep and dreamed of Mohawks swarmed by honeybees.

Memo from Agent Seagull Martin

Profile: Eve Brennan
Constable, St. Kilda Police Department
Date: Wednesday, December 10
Agent: Seagull Martin

The subject is approximately five foot
seven inches and weighs around 140
pounds (approx.). She is Caucasian, of
Scottish descent, but admits to having
possible gypsy on her grandmother's
side. She was born and bred in
Bundaberg but moved to Melbourne at
age sixteen after emancipating herself
from her parents. She worked for a
record company as a secretary and went
around in mohair jumpers and holey
tights. The subject said that when she
was a child, she dreamed of robbing big
corporations to give the money to the
poor. The subject is a pool shark. She
likes cats and has a ginger tabby called
Alvin Purple. The subject is a known
associate of Agent Bill Martin. She
worked as a barmaid at the Paradise
Theater and has allowed that Agent

Bill Martin used to wait around to
walk her home. She said sometimes he
would fall asleep waiting. The subject
still has family in Bundaberg—she
went back in the noughties after a
relationship breakup, and began doing
the community work which ultimately
led to her current employment at SKPD.
The subject's favorite food is enchiladas
and Lindt dark chocolate. She believes
that people are inherently good and that
public transport should be free. She has
no plans for Christmas.

ACTION
Agent Bill, ask her already!

CATSUITS AND WHIRLY-WINDS

OLD PEOPLE WORK FAST. Dad took Eve to the Berlin Bar party. Clothes came out of mothballs: second-generation stovepipe pants and pointy-toed boots, a shiny black jacket with leopard-skin lapels. Dad shaved his beard and pomped his hair and twist-toed down the stairs, snarling like Lux Interior. Vesna came over to babysit me and Gully. She found the Dunlops and poured Dad a long one. After he left, she looked wistful. She moved over to the window and watched Dad getting into Eve's car. She swirled the liquid in her glass. I could hear the soft rattle of her twenty-a-day habit.

"What's this one like?" she asked.

"Eve? She's nice. They're old friends. She's a cop."

Vesna's skimpy eyebrows went up so high they almost disappeared. She came back from the window and started straightening up, first herself, then the living room, then the kitchen. Finally she turned her attention to me. "You're getting pretty. You've got your dad's eyes. Have you got a boyfriend yet?"

I shook my head, but a smile snuck out. Vesna caught it.

"Who is he?"

"No one."

She grabbed my hands in a gesture of girlish community. "Ask me something. I've been around the block, but no one ever asks me anything."

"Okay. How do you know if a guy likes you?"

I'd asked Nancy the same question. She'd said if a guy liked you, his pupils would dilate. "When a dude gets those black marble eyes, he either wants to fuck you or he's stoned." She'd laughed her donkey-honk laugh. "Or both."

Vesna had a different take. She spoke to me with a scientist's precision. "A guy who likes you pays attention. You'll say something, and to you it'll just be a blip—inconsequential—but he'll take it and make it part of his woo."

"His woo?"

"Correct. I'm talking about his tools of seduction. Some guys use alcohol, some guys use flowers. Jimmy Irish used to take me to the dog track and let me pick, even though I always lost all his money. This guy— what's it like when you're alone together? Does he look at you? Talk to you?"

"He looks, but he's pretty quiet."

"He could be shy. Shy boys need a firm hand. Also— the element of surprise." Vesna patted my arm. "Oh, you look so worried. Don't be. Boys are like buses; if you miss one, another one will come along." Vesna stopped.

I could see her working backward, trying to figure out if she'd gotten the saying right. "Oh, what the hell. Boys are like buses, and if you get on the wrong one, you can always pull the cord."

The phone rang. I picked up.

"*Moshi moshi*, Sky!"

It was Mum. "*Moshi moshi,*" I echoed, moving up the stairs.

She launched into "Happy Birthday," giving it her best performance brass. I let her get all the way to the trilly end before stating, "My birthday's on Sunday."

There was an awesome trans-Pacific pause, and then she laughed lightly. "I knew that."

Mum's boyfriend, Yanni, joined in, "Hullo, Sky."

I was on speakerphone. I hated that.

Yanni talked like he'd learned English from a tape. "Galaxy's going to the Biennale. It's so exciting. We are all hammers and kettledrums."

Yanni was shiny-bald, but his back looked like a flokati rug. I witnessed his dodgy hair distro on our "family holiday," a year to the day after Mum first left. Japan was too expensive, so we met them in Penang. At the airport I said to Dad, "What if she kidnaps us?"

He looked stricken for a second. Then: "It's highly unlikely."

Polaroids from Penang: There was nothing to do but eat *gado gado*, and swim in the pool, and get laughed at by the busboys because I wore shorts instead of a bikini. Yanni spent the whole week on the phone, making deals. And then on the last night he loosened up. He gave me my first beer (vomit) and said girls who wear men's clothes are "like the sleeping hibiscus, they never unfurl" (vomit). At the karaoke club Mum made like Yoko Ono and nearly cleared the joint. An American boy named Chas Cheroot asked me to duet on "Somethin' Stupid"—and we lost Gully, only to find him back in the hotel room sorting through his collection of cocktail umbrellas. He had amassed four hundred in seven days, and had a major meltdown when Mum wouldn't let him take them home.

"How's school going?" Mum started on her list.

"Okay."

"How's Seagull?"

"He's still wearing the snout, if that's what you're asking."

She laughed. "I'd forgotten all about it."

"It's not funny. He wears it everywhere."

"What does he want for Christmas?"

"Night vision goggles."

"What about you?"

"What about me?"

Mum exhaled audibly. I pictured her in her blue *yukata*, smoking a poser cigarillo.

"So what are you doing for your birthday? Who are your friends, Sky? Have you found your people?"

Mum was always asking me if I'd found my people.

Yanni chimed in. "How's she supposed to know her people? She's only fifteen."

"Fifteen is *it*, Yanni," Mum cried. "Fifteen is when the world opens its *doors*."

"Does he have to listen in?" I complained.

There was silence. Then a click.

"Sky, what is going on? I'm hearing attitude." This was Mum trying to be perceptive. Trying. "Is this about a boy?"

"No."

"Is it about a girl?"

"Mum!"

"It's perfectly normal. It's nice to explore these things. . . ." She laughed again, a tinkly bell. I waited for wisdom, but none came. Mum started talking about her new performance and the catsuits and the whirly-winds. Blah blah blah.

I interrupted her. "Dad's got a new girlfriend. She looks like Ann-Margret."

"Oh, Sky, no one looks like Ann-Margret except Ann-Margret." I heard the click of her lighter. The sharp inhale. "Has he spoken to you about the shop?"

"No." My body tensed like it knew something bad was about to happen.

"I've sold it," Mum said.

Just like that. I nearly dropped the phone. My mouth fell open.

"Skylark? Are you still there?"

"Yes," I croaked.

"Of course your father was against it. I said to him, *What are you trying to hold on to?* I suppose it started when Yanni had the check for bowel cancer and I thought, we're not getting any younger. He's fine, by the way. So I kept saying no and they kept offering crazy money and then I said yes—and now here we are."

"But that doesn't make sense. He's just hired some-one."

"That's because your father's in denial."

My mouth was dry. I couldn't form words.

"I'm sure he'll tell you all about it." Mum started to say something else, but then Yanni said something in Greek and she replied back in Japanese. Her voice boomed in my ear. "I have to go—I have a sound check. *Oyasumi*, Sky."

"Oyasumi." I hung up and sat on my bed and stared dazedly around my bedroom. Mum had sold the shop, and Dad, who always told the truth, had somehow managed to let this one slip. I tried to process the information. Where were all those records going to go? Where were *we* going to go? If Mum had sold the shop, that meant the flat was probably next. Steve Sharp had bought the corner, just like Dad had said he would. I looked around at all of Mum's stuff: her bits and bobs and tchotchkes. Slowly, and then faster, I started to take

them down: the Noddy eggcup, the Mexican dancing girl, the lava lamp, the painting of the boy with the tear that was supposed to be cursed, the robot lunchbox, the matryoshka dolls, the peanut cushion, and the shell mobile. I filled every hatbox, every sky-blue vintage airport suitcase. I lined them up along my wall. I didn't do anything about her records or her clothes. I was mad, but I wasn't crazy.

Minus Mum's stuff, my room looked squattish, like it could have belonged to anyone. I closed my eyes. I could hear Vesna talking to Gully, and the soundtrack to *Joe 90* kicking in. The truth screamed above it: Mum had sold the shop. Dad knew, but he hadn't told us. When was he going to tell us? Clearly he was working the Martin family default: if we don't talk about it, it's not real. So maybe I could work it too.

I took the phone back downstairs. Gully was staring at the television. Vesna was picking something off the coffee table with scary intent.

"Everything okay?" she asked.

"Perfect," I said. My throat felt like someone was gripping it. I pinched the bridge of my nose in case any tears were working their way out, and then I wiped the slate of my mind clean and settled down to *Joe 90*.

Late in the night, in the yoga light, I listened to Leonard Cohen, but I didn't have to coax the sadness out. His voice was a long tunnel with the tiniest pinprick of light at the end. He managed to sound both near and faraway. Like, he could have been in the Hollywood Hills or hanging off my window ledge. Where were we going to go? What were we going to do? Outside the wind was blowing and the boat masts were singing. I let them sing me to sleep.

PART

THREE

Memo #3

A Memo from Agent Seagull Martin
Date: Friday, December 12
Agent: Seagull Martin
Address: 34 Blessington St., St. Kilda, upstairs

STATUS REPORT

POINT THE FIRST:

Constable Eve Brennan, SK PD, is still "looking into" the owners of registered white Jeeps in the local area *but* is unable to info-share.

POINT THE SECOND:

Recon #2 was a success. We now know that the white Jeep contained four young men. Further to that: the Jeep had a bumper sticker that read LOVE LIVE LOCAL.

POINT THE THIRD:

Nothing new on the CCTV.

IN SUMMATION

Not a lot of light shined this week, but I, Agent Seagull Martin, Special Investigations Unit, will persevere.

OTISWORLD

FRIDAY. I SAT IN the library staring at the GIF of my mother, hypnotized by her blank eyes and bloody nose. The black box popped up again. *Ask Me Anything!*

I typed, "How do you sleep?"

Quinn lurched in. "Hello, stranger."

She paused at my desk. Her bag dangled down, adorned with buttons and badges and band names. She slumped next to me and turned on her computer. Then she swiveled her chair to face mine. I saw her eyes light on my bead necklace.

"Sky*lark*," she said. "Nice."

From the neck up Quinn was after-five: her hair slicked back like some old glam rocker. She had shiny green eye shadow and bright red lipstick. She was wearing her glass bead necklaces too.

She said, "I went to Sydney. My grandma died."

"Sorry."

"It's okay. I didn't really know her."

She started to put her earbuds in. I grabbed her arm. I didn't want our conversation to end, but I didn't know how to keep it going.

"Uh, what's Sydney like?"

Quinn gave me a droll look. "Sydney's like . . . some bitch with shiny hair who keeps macking on your boyfriend."

"Right." I sat back in my chair. It crossed my mind that maybe the whole world was talking in code. Every day the list of what I didn't understand grew longer. I was two days away from turning sixteen, but I felt closer to six.

Quinn plugged her earbuds in and the usual cacophony sounded. She rocked in her chair and tapped her fingers on the keyboard, but after only half a minute she stopped, pulled her buds out. "What have you got next?"

"Social studies."

She grinned. "Shit. I can teach you that. You want to hang out?"

"Yes." The word flew from my lips, like it had been primed for weeks.

Quinn's eyebrows bounced above her frosty greens. "Cool."

Hanging out with Quinn meant watching her change at the bus shelter. Her uniform had Velcro attachments so she could rip it off like a stripper—only she wasn't hiding pasties, she was hiding a cherry-red bowling shirt and cutoffs. It meant walking down the Windsor end of Chapel Street, drinking coffee and looking in thrift shops. It meant watching her fist-bump skeevy bums near the mission and admiring her swagger and wondering how she got to cultivate a walk like that. Quinn talked loudly and said "fuck" a lot. And every now and then I'd catch her looking at me, like she was checking to see that I was having a good time. And I was.

We ended up at her house, the upstairs of a red-brick two-story covered in ivy. She paused at the first step as if unsure I would follow, but I was so on her tail I crashed into her. She led me into a spare, neat flat. There were books and pot plants and rag rugs. "Boring," Quinn said as she walked. She led me down a hallway and unlocked her bedroom door. It was like walking into a nightclub with the sound turned down. Her bedroom had licorice walls and stick-on stars everywhere. She hit her light switch and for a moment everything went silver. Then my eyes adjusted to the mirrors, the shiny filing cabinets, the black-and-white photographs that hung in strips from silver threads like an elaborate web.

"Wow," I said. "Don't your parents hate it?"

"It's only my mum. She says it's my space."

"Where's your dad?"

"He has another family." Quinn shrugged. "His loss."

I couldn't help comparing Quinn's bedroom to mine. It was all her. It screamed Quinn Bishop. What did my room say? Especially now, with Mum's stuff in bags. The only things in my room that said anything about me were embarrassing—like the box of beautiful people. Except for my records. Maybe my records were all I was. For a moment I felt a shiver and remembered that Mum had sold the shop, but I pushed the feeling away. I could do that.

Quinn sat on her bed. I sat next to her. She reached beside me for her laptop and tapped and clicked. Then she put the machine on my lap. "Enjoy."

I was looking at a website with party photos.

"What is it?" I asked, starting to slowly scroll down.

"It's Otisworld, don't you know?" She frowned. "How did you end up at the gig?"

"Steve Sharp brought tickets into the shop."

"You know Steve Sharp?"

"He's a customer."

The images were different from the ones the week before, but the theme was the same. Parties. Girls. Mess and noise. The pictures could have been taken twenty years in the past or the future: club girls, cool girls, drunk girls, nude girls, all staring down the lens with expressions that ranged between hostile and ecstatic.

"I wasn't even going to go," I said. "It was Nancy."

"Who's Nancy?"

Just as Quinn said her name, I saw her. Agent Nancy Cole, KGB. There were two pictures of her side by side. In the first she was standing on a balcony, leaning with her elbows back on the rail and a *fuck you* look on her face. She wore an oversize T-shirt, nothing else. In the second photo she was in the same pose but naked. I felt my face burn. In a voice that didn't sound like mine I said, "That's Nancy."

Quinn was not shocked at naked Nancy. She assessed the pictures, like she would any art, and scrolled on. She came to a picture of a girl lying back on the grass, laughing. Next to her face was a horse's head. The picture was jarring—at first glance it looked like the horse was her Siamese twin.

"That's one of mine," Quinn said proudly.

"Why don't they credit you?"

"The whole point is it's anonymous."

"Where'd you take it?"

"A mess last year. Wait. You don't know what a mess is either, do you?" I shook my head and stared at the screen. I could hear my breath coming shallow. Quinn rolled her fingers over her necklaces and launched into my education.

"Okay, so a mess is a private party for the cognoscenti. That's me. And now you. Maybe. Usually what happens is Otis plays and there's DJs and, ah, refreshments. You know that tunnel under Inkerman Street— used to be around for bootleggers? They had a mess there last year. Forty-something mess-heads dancing under the traffic, and no one even knew."

"Who organizes them?"

"No one knows. They don't start until late. And they only disclose the location at the last minute." Quinn turned back to the screen. "The photos come from the messes, but people also send them in, in the spirit of the messes."

I continued scrolling past Otis photosets: stage shots of him writhing on pallets. Did I want to see older posts? Almost certainly. The photos were dark and strange; they looked professionally amateur. I saw animal masks, a face through a gauzy silver scarf, and a tribute to Jimi Hendrix's *Electric Ladyland*—a garden of girls in their underpants. Boobs out, boots on, silver scarves, deadpan faces. I froze. The girl in the back with her face half-hidden beneath her hair was Mia Casey. I was certain.

"Do you know her?" I asked.

Quinn paused. "I heard she was at a mess before she died."

"The papers said she was at the Paradise."

"I heard she was at a mess," Quinn repeated. "She got gypped. She got too into it. There are a lot of girls like her."

"The ones with the silver scarves?"

Quinn nodded.

"What does it mean if Nancy's got a scarf?"

"It means she's fucking Otis." Quinn smiled. "Personally, I wouldn't go there. I couldn't go out with a guy who was smaller than me. Also, who wants to be a number?"

Quinn's face changed then. She went from tough to

soft, just like that. The way she was looking at me made me feel heavy. "I wasn't really in Sydney," she said. "I was in the hospital. I have to go in sometimes. For my head. You think I'm a freak now, right? I don't care."

I smiled hesitantly. "I like freaks."

Downstairs a door opened and closed. Quinn slammed her laptop shut. "That's my mum."

"What time is it?"

"Three fifteen."

"Shit. I've got to get my brother."

I was trying to work out the best way to say goodbye, and then Quinn swooped in for a hug. Our bead necklaces clashed. Her voice vibrated in my ear, "I knew we were going to be friends."

NOTHING OR SOMETHING

GULLY WAS SITTING IN the gutter with his head in a paperback called *Secrets of the MI5*. My shadow blocked his light. He spoke without looking up.

"You're late."

"I know."

We started walking. Gully was hanging his head like it was so heavy his neck couldn't support it. Something bad had happened. Some little arsehole had said something or done something. In Gully's class there were a few victims; it was like the bullies had them on rotation. I probed Gully. He shuffled his feet, took a while to answer.

"Jack Pratt pantsed me."

"Did anyone do anything?"

"Laughed. And did this." He held his pinkie finger acrook.

I put my arm around him; he froze, and I retracted it. "Pratt by name, prat by nature. They're dickheads. All of them, dickheads."

Gully half smiled. "Mouth."

We crossed the highway and tripped along St.

Kilda's wide and leafy backstreets. Everything looked different somehow. Like a layer had been stripped off the world. I felt tremulous, on the edge, but also weirdly happy. I shunned the new townhouses with their manicured gardens and gave all my love to the fifties flats with their pockmarked plane trees giving shade to the shady. The wind was blowing and the palms were swaying. The sun felt sharp-hot on my skin.

Someone wolf-whistled. "Hey, girlfriend!"

Nancy was perched on an old armchair that had been shifted onto the nature strip. I saw the silver scarf first, and then the photograph flashed in my mind. She sprang over to us and then stood there, slightly out of breath. In addition to the scarf, Nancy was wearing a floppy black hat and sunglasses and a man's business shirt over cutoffs.

"Are you incognito?" Gully covered his mouth with his hand, spy-talking.

Nancy bent to his height and spy-talked back. "Affirmative!"

She moved so I could clock the contents of her bag: two bottles of champagne. "Courtesy of the Purple Onion. Let's get stinko."

I took Gully by the shoulders. "I've got to check in with Agent Cole, KGB, talk turkey, get intel, you savvy?"

"I want to come too."

"You can't."

"Why not?"

"Because we're going to be talking about periods," Nancy said loudly.

Gully went red. His lip trembled like he was about to cry. "Hey! I'm joking," Nancy said, but Gully was already trudging away. After a few steps he turned back. "What about fish and chips?"

I waved him off. "Tell Dad to start without me."

The greenhouse was jungle-steamy; the perfect place for an assignation, if that was what we were having. Nancy and I collapsed on the bench and smiled at each other. My stomach flip-flopped. She took a bottle out of her bag and popped the cork. It flew up and I imagined it shattering the ceiling and glass raining down, skewering the goldfish and making the paving slabs sing. This didn't happen. What did happen was I took a gulp and the drink went down the wrong pipe and came back up through my nose. Nancy drank like Dad on a bad night, like she'd been crawling across the desert for infinite days. She set the bottle down and released an epic burp.

"Your turn," she said, like that constituted conversation.

Where to start? Otis and the photograph, Luke and the Fugg, Quinn Bishop and messes, the Ugly Mugs, the elusive Bricker, the sale of the shop, the end of the world.

I started with Mum's phone call.

"That's tough," Nancy said. But her voice rang hollow. She didn't get it—she had no family, she moved around. She was like that Rolling Stones song "Ruby Tuesday"—I used to think it was exotic, but now I wasn't so sure. If you lived like that, what was to stop you from disappearing altogether?

I took a swig of champagne and rushed on to the next item. "So my friend Quinn showed me this website, called Otisworld, and it's photos of . . . stuff . . . but mostly girls." I paused. "You're on it."

Nancy put her hand to her heart. "Me?" But this was wrong; she looked surprised and flattered.

I nodded.

"Doing what?"

I swallowed. "Okay. You're naked."

She waved her hand. "Oh, that. He put that up?"

I stared at her.

"What?" She rattled my wrist. "What?"

"Don't you care? Don't you care that you're naked and it's online and anyone can see?"

"First of all, not just anyone can see. You have to have a password. And no one who *knows me* is going to look at that. And even if they did, so what? When I'm forty and my arse is sagging somewhere down around my ankles, I'm going to be able to look back and say, *I used to be something*."

"But it makes you look like nothing. Put like that,

with the pictures all rolling one after the other, it makes you look like nothing."

"Sky, it's really not a big deal."

I felt confused. Was it nothing, or was it something? Then I remembered Mia.

"There was a picture of Mia Casey, too. It was from earlier. She was with a group of girls. She had a scarf."

I checked Nancy's neck. The lovebites were still there but faded. They looked like brown summer blossoms, like the end of something. Nancy was looking at me like she felt sorry for me. She clucked. "Poor dollbaby. Don't you know, the road of excess leads to the palace of wisdom? Jim Morrison said that." She leaned in. For a second I thought she was going to kiss me again. A pause like a canyon yawped between us, and then she laughed her donkey-honk laugh and I ducked my head, embarrassed that I was always getting so lost in her.

After that we fell quiet. Nancy smacked my arm and I smacked hers back. We went back and forth like that a few rounds. She took off her black hat and put it on my head, and then she stood, stretched, and sighed. She grabbed an overhanging palm frond and fanned herself with it, affecting the air of a jaded chanteuse.

"So, how is Otis?" I asked.

"He's beautiful. He's my soul mate."

"Seriously?"

"No." A crooked smile. "Let me tell you about Otis Sharp: He looks hot, but the guy has *isshews*. Number one: he can't hold his drink. Number two: he's more interested in looking than doing. Hence photo. Number three: he cries, like, all the time. You thought that was just part of the show, right? Well, let me tell you, it's real. Number four: his fat friend? Om-ni-pres-ent."

She lit a cigarette and exhaled a gray cloud.

"So, you're not in love?"

"Dollbaby, love is a fiction. Love is, like, those pictures from the seventies with the kids and the flares and the big moony eyes. Of course I'm not in love. I'm working an angle."

I laughed, but Nancy looked serious. The way she talked, it was like all those movies she'd watched had seeped into her system. I couldn't tell when she was quoting and when she was being herself. I should have been feeling relieved. Otis meant nothing, and summer could go back to being summer—but even as I thought this, I knew it was all wrong.

Nancy snapped the branch of the palm. It made a sharp cracking sound. She said, "That party I went to with Ray. Your dad was there with some foxy redhead, looking very loved-up."

"That's Eve," I said faintly.

"And that reminds me." She dug in her bag and brought out a piece of paper. "For your dad."

Dear Bill,

I'm writing to apologize for not looking out for Sky when we went out last Friday night. Sky's my good friend and I'm not used to having good friends, but that's not really an excuse. I let you down and her down, and for this I'm truly sorry. I hope you'll let me take her out for her birthday— nothing crazy, I promise. Just two grand old girls having a grand old time.

Nancy

"Okay?" she asked.

I looked at her, feeling weird. "Okay."

She opened the second bottle and passed it along. I was already woozy, but I kept drinking. And the more I drank, the less weird I felt. Then we were laughing again, and nothing was serious and we were in the moment and the moment was everything. Outside, the sky grew dark; birds were convening in the fig tree. Nancy's phone pinged and she had to lam. I weaved along the path, gulping air. The grass in the dark looked like velvet. I lay upon it and stared up at the sky. The stars were spinning. I might have hugged a palm tree before puking.

Back at the flat Dad and Gully were playing Jenga. I pulled out a chair a little too forcefully, and the tower trembled. They froze. Dad kept his eyes on the block he was trying to pry out of the pile. "Where have you been?"

"At the gardens."

"You're supposed to see Gully all the way home."

"He only had to walk two blocks. He's not five.

"You have to tell me when you're going out."

"I was being spontaneous."

The tower remained. A triumph.

Dad said, "You missed fish and chips."

Missing fish and chips was tantamount to treason.

"I wasn't hungry." *You let Mum sell the shop.* I thought it, but I didn't say it.

Dad eyeballed me. "Have you been drinking?"

"No!" I snorted. "Have you?"

I could stare Dad out—his right eye started twitching after three seconds. He looked down.

"Nice hat," he muttered.

I thrust Nancy's letter at him.

Dad read it and put it on the table next to his glass.

"Sky, Sky." Gully was touching my arm. "Sky, Sky, Sky—"

"What?"

"I ate your flake. It was good."

CRAZY PEOPLE

I WAS HUNGOVER AGAIN. I was beginning to see how Dad could get used to it. The headache was bracing, but the floating feeling that went with it was almost pleasant. I felt wispy, insubstantial, like the world was spinning but I was standing off to the side. The feeling stayed with me as I dressed; it followed me to breakfast, where the idea of food was ridiculous. I drank water and watched Gully hunched over some project, humming as he worked. The air around him felt frenetic. I had to sit down. I put my hand in my pocket, and my fingers felt something—Luke's wristband. I slipped it on my wrist and promptly forgot about it.

"Gully, what are you doing?"

"I'm making a sign."

He flashed the cardboard.

WANTED: INFORMATION
Do you own or have you seen a white Jeep?
Sticker on the back says love live local.
Come into the Wishing Well, ask for Agent

*Seagull Martin, Special Investigations
Unit, in collaboration with SKPD. Reward.*

"What's the reward?"

"There's no reward," Gully replied. "That's the bait."

"Clever."

"I know."

"What are you going to do when you find the Bricker?"

"Make a citizen's arrest. Hand him over to SKPD."

"Let me put it another way: What are you going to do if you *don't* find him?"

But Gully didn't want to hear that. He hummed louder. He filled in the block letters that had already been filled. The humming and his hand moving up and down did something to me. I reached over and put my hand on his. I pressed hard.

"HEY!" Gully cried. "Don't do that."

Dad appeared in the doorway. "What's going on?"

I took my hand back. "Nothing."

Dad moved around me to the coffeepot. He poured a cup and sipped at it, his eyes never leaving my face.

"Is there something you want to tell me, Sky?"

"No. Is there something *you* want to tell *me*?"

Dad looked at Gully. "Gully, can you excuse us?"

Gully gathered his work and huffed off to the living room.

Dad hunched across the table. He had Things To Say. I braced myself.

"Skylark. Last night. Not good. You're supposed to be grounded. And I don't want you drinking."

"I wasn't drinking."

"I think I have some experience in this area."

I looked at him straight.

"I want to go out for my birthday."

"I can't stop you."

"You could try trusting me. How am I supposed to find my people if I don't go out anywhere?"

Dad's eyes narrowed. "Your people?"

"Mum's always saying, *Have you found your people?* You found yours. Eve said you had a whole gang. But all I've got is Nancy, so you should cut me some slack."

"Maybe you're right." Dad sighed. He put his coffee cup in the sink and looked around. The kitchen had gone back to its bombsite state. He gave me a bleak smile and offered his arms up for a hug. I resisted. Was he going to tell me about the shop? I stared at him, willing him to tell me. I tried telepathy. *I know. I know Mum sold us down the river.* It didn't work.

When Dad spoke, it was about something else. "I need you to mind the shop with Luke. I've got to go see a man about some records. I'll take Gully."

"What about my sign?" Gully shouted. He'd been listening all along.

"Sky will put it up for you. Won't you?"

I raised my eyebrows.

Dad gave my arm a squeeze. The brief moment of contact put me off-balance. It was like he was squeezing my heart. He said, "If anyone's selling, tell them to come back."

"What's the point?" I muttered under my breath. It was galling, how Dad could act like everything was normal. I understood why he didn't want to tell Gully about the shop being sold—Gully had a shit fit if we so much as drove a different way home—but he could have told me. Now my head was pounding. My mouth felt dry. I felt shaky, seedy, and that floating feeling had disappeared, replaced with bitterness.

Alone with Luke, on a Saturday. I tried to remember Vesna's advice—the firm hand, the element of surprise— but then Nancy's voice kept crashing the party: *You don't have to do anything to make a guy think about sex because he's already thinking it.*

Luke was waiting out front. He didn't look like he was thinking about sex. He looked worried. I gave him a terse nod and turned the key in the lock. Once inside, I turned off the alarm and flicked the lights—we had two and a half fluorescent bars working; the other half stuttered and threshed like a dying moth. I went through to the back room and opened that door to let some air in. I counted out the float. Without music the shop was too quiet. I flicked through my holds stash for something to play and decided on Bert Jansch—his voice was sullen and spare. It always made me feel sad, but I didn't mind feeling sad that morning. As I performed my menial tasks, Luke stood with his back to me, gazing up at the Wall of Woe. I slammed the till tray shut to get his attention.

"It's just you and me today. Dad has to see a man about some records."

Luke came around the counter. I went on speaking without looking at him.

"That doesn't actually mean he's going to see a man about some records. It just means he's not coming in." I paused. "At least he took snout-boy. I'm supposed to put *this* up." I indicated Gully's sign, and then I caught Luke's eye and kept it. "Have *you* seen a white Jeep, Luke?"

He shook his head. He was looking at me so seriously. His eyes were hazy blue behind his glasses. It was unnerving, the way he looked at me. I felt darkness inside, the drama rising in me.

"Crazy people," I said. "My dad and Gully, they're cracked." I glared at Luke. "Why don't you talk?"

Luke mumbled, "What do you want me to say?"

"Something. Anything. I don't even know why you're here."

"Well, I'm working."

"Right," I said. I stared down at the counter, at the wood grain, the million pencil marks. There was a long arc of silence, and then Luke cleared his throat. "My sister was crazy."

He wasn't smiling. He gave a slight shrug and rubbed his hands across his knees. He spoke slowly, like he was rolling the words around his mouth before sending them out to that place where once said, they couldn't be taken back.

"Mia was hard work. When we were kids, I never knew if she wanted to hug me or fight me. I don't think she knew either. She broke my arm when I was eight. But she also put a hex on every bully who ever tried anything. That was during her high-priestess phase. She had a poet phase too, and she dabbled in pharmaceuticals. I don't know where she got her ideas from or why certain things held and certain things didn't. When I strike a match, I think about her. The flare and the hiss and the way the flame dies down quick, but your fingers still sting afterward." He ducked his head. "I don't have very good memories of her. I think she had, like, a self-destruct button. She'd been running away since she was twelve. And everything else. In the end it was like we just let her go. Mum used to put money in her account, but it was never enough. I know this sounds bad, but I wasn't surprised when I heard she was dead. I was only surprised it hadn't happened sooner."

Maybe if we'd been facing each other, Luke wouldn't have spoken, but parallel as we were, talking seemed easier. I could imagine we were strangers on a train, turning our stories along with the wheels.

He outlined incidents, his voice thick, almost hypnotic: Fights. Boys. Drugs. Homes. Hope. Heartbreak. His words made me feel like I didn't know anything. And after this outpouring Luke sat staring straight ahead, his hands curled into fists. The muscle on his cheek pulsed.

"Our surname, Casey, it's supposed to mean watchful and vigilant, but I wasn't much good at either. The way you are with Gully—it's really special. It makes me wish I could go back and change everything." His eyes traveled down; at the same time we both realized I was wearing his wristband.

"I found it, when I was cleaning up."

"It's okay," Luke said. "You can have it."

Silence again. He took a deep breath through his nostrils and released it. "Anyway. I didn't answer your question. I'm here because . . . well . . . my parents didn't want an inquiry. They just wanted to bring Mia home, but I felt like . . . I feel like . . ."

Luke never finished what he was going to say because just then the door opened and two people walked in. It was Otis Sharp followed by Rocky. My hackles went up. Otis didn't know me; he didn't know that I knew anything about him and Nancy and the penthouse and the lovebites. He didn't know I'd seen him crying after the attack of the Paradise protestors.

He was shorter than I remembered, but still with that wayward kind of glamour. His hair was terrifically shaggy, and his black jeans were dead tight. He wore white leather shoes and a cowhide vest, and the whole look was expensive but careless.

Rocky lumped a box on the counter.

"I'm selling."

Luke leaned forward to match Rocky's aggro.

"The buyer's not here."

"It's okay," I said. "I can do it."

Rocky watched me as I went through the buy. His presence made me rush, and I could only remember two of Dad's rules: Move fast. Keep a poker face.

The records were good. If they'd been terrible, the buy would have been easier. For some I had to check the pricing guide. For everything else I erred on the side of generosity.

I was halfway through when Otis erupted into a giggle fit. Rocky didn't look at him, but I could see muscles tense on his hands. Otis stopped giggling, sighed, and started giggling again. He was stoned. I had a moment of not-quite fear. Once a guy had pulled a syringe on Dad, but he'd been so wobbly he couldn't aim straight, and Dad had shamed him out of the shop.

Rocky leaned farther over the counter.

"That's not going to make her any quicker," Luke said.

"Who asked you?" Rocky snapped.

I glanced up at him and then to where Otis was standing in a shaft of light, staring dazedly down, rubbing his chest, making the cowhide crackle. And then I readied the stack. "Seventy-five cash or ninety tr—"

"CASH." Rocky spoke over me.

"Someone's in a hurry," I muttered to Luke as he handed over the Buys Book. I asked for ID and Rocky gave me his license. I smirked at the photo, the way Dad always did, and jotted down his details. Then I counted out the money.

Rocky passed the wad to Otis, who put it in a money clip that was already pretty hefty. Otis snapped his fingers. "Let's go, Rocky Raccoon."

They left, slamming the door behind them so hard that the Barry Manilow cover with the speech bubble that said NO ID NO BUY plummeted to the floor.

Luke looked at me. "Nice guys."

"Good records." I shrugged. Patti Smith's *Easter* stared at me from the top of the pile. I put it on. It was all pent-up-ness and yearning.

Luke picked up the box. "Should I put them out back?"

"Yes." I said, then: "No!"

Luke waited with the box in his arms.

Suddenly I felt nervous. Dad was going to be shitty. Why had I thought I could buy? But there was no going back now. I'd even written it in the book. In my hungover daze and panic I made a decision. While Luke was out back, I ripped the page with Rocky's deets out of the Buys Book and stuffed it in my pocket. For the next half hour I sat there scheming about how I could make the box disappear before Dad returned. In the end I simply reclaimed the box and lugged it up to my room. I put it next to the bin-bags of Mum's stuff. Then I went to the bathroom and took a Tylenol. I washed my face and brushed my teeth. The last thing I saw before I walked out was my paper effigies of Nancy, Otis, and me and Luke, me, and Mia. Crazy Mia. *Well,* her eyes seemed to say, *you wanted to know, and now you do.*

UNDER THE SEA

HE DAY ROLLED SLOW. Luke didn't talk anymore. He sat sketching while I wandered the shop floor, straightening the racks. I liked the records to all be leaning back, facing me, full of promise. As I looked at their shiny faces, I felt a mixture of awe and sadness. Music was everything: the whole stinging, ringing pulse of being human was in here. Even the g-sale stock, even Barry Gibb and Barbra Streisand.

How could we give it up? Music was memory, too. I could hear Jan and Dean doing "Pocketful of Rainbows" and be rocketed back to Mum pacing the flat with Gully in a sling. I could play "Incense and Peppermints" and revisit Nancy hippie-dancing in a Glomesh headband. If I really wanted to feel wistful, I could play Johnny Rivers's "Secret Agent Man," which was Gully's theme song back when the spy stuff was cute and not evidence of dodgy neural wiring.

Luke took his turn on the stereo. We were back to Simon & Garfunkel. This time I knew better than to comment. I even turned the volume up so that I could drown out my thoughts. "The Boxer" came on and it was plaintive and forlorn and like the soundtrack for the few customers trundling around the shop. One hanging around World Music started singing along atonally. I smiled. I could feel Luke smiling too. I watched him sketch from the corner of my eye and I wondered if he was sketching me. After a minute he nudged the sketch-book across two inches so that it was right in front of me. I looked down and saw the customers. Luke's rendering was realistic, tragi-comic. It was all there: arse cracks and adenoids, thinning pates and perfect recall of *Countdown* episodes; fifty-year-old men eating TV dinners with their mothers.

"You're good," I told him.

Luke shrugged, but I detected a glow. I tried to drag it out. "So, is this what you see yourself doing?"

"Sketching sad little men?"

"No . . ." I blushed. "Art, I don't know." Weren't you supposed to ask guys about their interests? Wasn't that the way in? "I'm just trying to get to know you," I muttered.

Luke glanced up. Maybe he could see he'd hurt my feelings. "You're sweet."

"No. I'm not."

"Yeah. You are."

He stood up and shook his long legs out and did a circuit of the shop, coming to rest at Cardboard Elvis.

I pitched my voice above the music. "Gully says if

you look into his eyes, you can see the future."

But Luke wasn't looking at Elvis's eyes; he was staring at the Wishing Well cassettes. He picked one up. "Do a lot of people buy these?"

"If by a lot you mean half a dozen, then yes."

He reached into his back pocket and brought out a cassette tape. It had our logo on it and a symbol: three lines meeting, like a primitive rake.

"This was in my sister's stuff."

"What's on it?"

"Weird shit. Old songs. I don't know anything about music, remember?"

"I saw you listening to it."

"When?"

I answered without thinking. "CCTV."

Luke looked at me, looked away, then looked at me again.

"I was looking for the white Jeep!" I protested. But we both knew I was lying. And suddenly it struck me: how much I'd seen. How much I'd already speculated upon. I thought about the photograph of Mia on Otisworld. I didn't know what Luke knew, but I wasn't about to introduce the subject now.

"Can I hear it?" I asked.

Luke looked around, unsure. Then he handed me the tape. I put it in the player. The Buzzcocks came on like a preteen with a power drill. Luke was picking up the Wishing Well tapes and putting them down again.

Somehow he managed to dislodge the tray. Cardboard Elvis toppled and the tapes scattered over the counter and floor. I crouched to pick them up, and then we were both down there. That moment, under the counter, was like being under the sea, and realizing you can breathe underwater. Our hands brushed as we reached for the same tape at the same time. Our eyes met and I clumsily leaned over and kissed him. Luke's lips felt cool. He didn't do anything for a second, and then he kissed me back. Smoke and Polo mints, stuff unsaid. It was more than nice. It made me feel weightless, adrift, but then Gully's voice booming, high above sea level, reeled me back in.

"Guys—where are you?"

Luke and I emerged, miles apart, red-faced. We had failed to gather the Wishing Well cassettes, and Cardboard Elvis lay at an awkward angle, still smiling, always smiling. Dad was standing behind Gully, looking perturbed. "What's going on?"

"Nothing."

Gully shook his head at the fallout. "You've made a real mess." He scanned the shop. "Where's my sign?"

"I haven't put it up yet."

Luke pressed the stop button and slipped the tape back in his pocket. Then he shoved a cigarette in his mouth and walked outside with his head low.

I watched him out there, leaning one foot back

against the plane tree, smoking and radiating sadness. When he came back in, he acted as if nothing had happened. I couldn't help thinking I'd wrecked things somehow. If I were Nancy, this wouldn't have happened. If I were Nancy, we'd still be down there.

LOVE LIVE LOCAL

I T WAS MARTIN FAMILY tradition to leave presents behind the door of the birthday person. On Sunday morning I opened mine to find a card and a parcel. The card was handmade with a sketch of Gully and me on stakeout—but it was way too professional to be my brother's handiwork. He still did stick figures. Knowing that Luke had drawn the picture made me feel slightly thrilled and slightly sick. He'd drawn me even prettier than last time. I checked my reflection in the mirror, but if some magic transformation had happened, I couldn't see it.

I opened the card.

Agent Skylark Martin,
You are now sixteen. Under Victorian law you are legally allowed to fornicate (as long as your partner isn't more than two years older or your legal guardian). You can get your ears, nose, and cheeks pierced without a note from your parents. You can attain a probationary driver's license (I recommend this). If the police want to search you

*for whatever reason, they are limited to patting
you down. You can't leave home legally, but,
should you choose to, as long as you can prove
you're not in serious danger, the cops will walk
soft. I hope this information is helpful. And that
you have a great day.*

Affectionately yours,

Agent Seagull Martin (Gully)

I unwrapped the parcel to find the *Nuggets*
compilation—Dad didn't mind if *I* cheated—twenty-
four psych-rock freak-outs by bands with names like
Mouse and the Magic Mushrooms. I put on side one and
lurched about to the jangly guitars and schizophrenic
drums. I was thinking about Luke. It was Gully's card
that did it. *I can have sex with Luke Casey—he's eighteen, so it's okay.* Not that we had to go straight from
zero to sixty. There was a world of things we could do. I
accessed my mind file of Nancy's Kama Sutra, changing
the faces to fit Luke's and mine. I imagined him kissing me and kissing me and kissing me. Luke Casey's
tongue would not be sandpapery or slimy. I would not
be able to taste what he'd had for lunch.

I considered my wardrobe, returning to the green
dress. I added the bead necklace, Luke's wristband,
and Nancy's hat.

We moseyed to the gardens and found our bench.
I was lost in Luke-land. Every time an unpleasant

thought popped up, I papered over it with the memory of Luke's face just before he kissed me. *You're sweet,* he said it on a loop, and it didn't sound so sucky.

It was a gray day. There were plenty of gaps in the market line. The Fugg was there, but I couldn't see Ray. I checked my phone. There was nothing from Nancy—no birthday greeting, no invite to a wild night out. I wondered if she'd forgotten. My mind returned to Luke—Luke reaching to reposition a lock of my hair. Meanwhile, Gully pulled the tomato out of his toastie and flung it to the seagulls. One came and then twenty, and he became overwhelmed and had to bury his head in his hands. But he wasn't vanquished for long. When he came back up, he had his notebook out. He made the fist. *Chh!*

"Date: Sunday, December fourteenth. Time: 0935 hours. Location: O'Donnell Gardens. House Meeting Actioned."

There was a huge pause.

Dad looked at Gully. "Item?" he coached, but Gully was somewhere else, his blue eyes staring into the distance. All of a sudden he was up and running. Dad groaned. "What now?" I threw down my toastie and hurried after him.

He'd stopped at the entrance to Luna Park. He was staring at a sign, his face frozen. I saw what he saw: the sign, the stack of flyers.

LOVE LIVE LOCAL—TONIGHT 6 PM—OTIS, THE BIG
RACKET, MOMO—FREE ENTRY. ALL AGES.

Gully turned to me, his face incandescent. He
drummed his finger over his snout, fast in the manner
of Monkey.

"We have to go!" he shouted.

I took a step back and shook my head. "Sorry. It's
my birthday. I've got plans."

"Change them." Gully bolted back to Dad. I followed slowly, feeling as if my feet were sinking with
each step. Nancy's absence nagged at me. I could see
Gully pleading and wheedling. Bill the Patriarch and
traitor kept trying to catch my eye, but I refused to let
him.

"Sky?"

"What if I don't want to go? What if I have other
plans?"

"Well, do you?"

I turned away. I could see the edge of Mia where
Luke had been busted pasting her up. All that remained
was one black eye and three black tears.

"I suspect the Bricker will be there," Gully said.

"I. Don't. Care."

"Sky!" Dad scolded. "What's the matter with you?"

I could think of a few things: my best friend had
gone AWOL, my mother was a bitch, my dad was a liar,
and my brother was a kook.

I checked my phone again. It was like a dead

thing in my hand. I started punching out a text to Nancy. "Are we going out, or what?" but then I deleted it. I didn't need to look in Elvis's eyes to know what lay ahead. I was going to Luna Park with my crazy brother, in search of a mythical white Jeep. Happy birthday to me.

At the shop I avoided Luke's eyes. I stayed on the back counter with my head in *Record Collector*, and now I let all the thoughts in: I thought about Otis's records planted in my room. I thought about Nancy posing naked on penthouse balconies. I thought about Quinn saying, "She got gypped," and I thought, she could have been talking about me. Gully chattered the day away, filling Luke in about the Bricker. He gave him a flyer. "LOVE LIVE LOCAL!" He said it like a mantra. "You can come too!"

Luke looked at me; his lips hid a smile. "Maybe I will." And for the first time I felt a crack in the gloom.

But Nancy turned up after all. At five to six she burled through the door all lit up like an oil refinery. She had the biker boots, the spandex, the tiny black vest. And the scarf—of course, the scarf. It caught the light like sparks off a side grinder.

"Happy birthday, Sky!" Nancy came around the counter and squeezed between me and Dad and Gully. We were in the middle of negotiations for the night ahead. Luke came out from the back room. I saw him clock Nancy. His eyes opened a tad wider and he didn't look away.

"Who's the bright boy?" Nancy asked, sounding for all the world like a gangster's moll.

"That's Luke," Dad said.

"What's his angle?" She cracked a smile. "Just kidding. Hi, I'm Nancy. I've heard about you." She held out her hand, not to shake but to kiss. It was a jokey-presumptuous gesture. Nancy was playing for laughs, but Luke still had the stares. Nancy turned to me, arced an eyebrow, then moved on, clapping her hands. "Let's go, little sister."

"Hold on, go where?"

"I'm taking you out, remember?"

Gully cut in, giving Nancy the full snout. "Agent Skylark has other commitments. This is *big*, Agent Cole. This is a *breakthrough!*"

"Calm down," Dad ordered. *"Calm."*

"We're going to Luna Park," I explained. "You never rang, so I thought—"

"Synchronicity!" Nancy cried. "That's where *I* was going to take *you!*"

"Now, hold on," Dad said. "What's happening here?"

"I think we're all going," I said. "Is that okay?"

How could he refuse? He gave me a fifty from the till. "Look after your brother." To Gully he said, "Stay with your sister. No going rogue."

"I won't." Gully raced for the door. I followed, and at the last minute flung a look at Luke that was as good as a wave forward.

"Is he coming?" Nancy sounded confused. She winched my arm as we walked out. "What's going *on*?" she hissed. "Are you two—"

"Shut *up!*"

"Okay." She pressed her lips into a sort of smile.

"I thought you were over Otis," I said.

"It's different when he plays."

When we reached the gardens, Nancy dive-bombed Gully to the grass and tickled him, until he was just a blur of snout and gap teeth and half-moon eyes. Gully's laugh was like helium, or the first dip on the Scenic Railway. I tumbled down next to them. We lay in the grass, silent, breathless. Clouds rolled fast across the sky. And I remember thinking, beautiful things move fast.

RECON #3: LUNA PARK

AD CALLED LUNA PARK the Mouth of Hell. This was because if you hadn't been seduced by the tizz and cotton candy, if you looked with clear eyes, you'd see it as it was: ugly, aimless, noisy, tacky. I stood at the ticket booth and watched Nancy work her magic. The guy didn't have a prayer, but he held her wrist anyway, shouting against the din that he got off at nine.

"Awesome!" Nancy shouted back. She smiled big and fake and walked away. She got a lot of twice-overs. Guys drooled; girls clawed up.

"What's it like?" I asked her.

"What's what like?"

"Having guys look at you all the time."

"I don't even see them, dollbaby." But her eyes shifted left. "Sometimes if the guy's really ugly, I smile at him. Because you've got to have some hope in the world."

"That's nice," I said. "You're like a community service."

She put her palms out. "I do what I can."

Luke and Gully were waiting for us. Gully had his

head cocked, snout at the fore, tool belt primed. His plan to stalk the car park first crumpled in the face of the bumper cars. At the southern end a stage was set up, the sign prominent: LOVE LIVE LOCAL. Roadies tooled around trailing cords. A group of girls was hovering. Two of them wore silver scarves. They huddled and murmured and sent dirty looks in our direction. Luke looked perturbed. His eyes sought mine and he gave me a lost sort of smile. Nancy grabbed Gully's hand. Luke and I followed.

Gully was fearless on the bumper cars. Meat-faced dudes raged at him, but he just set his jaw and turned to the next collision. Nancy was laughing hard. I watched her head jerking around. When the siren came, she kissed Gully full on the mouth and his face went bright red. Something like jealousy swept all my corners. Luke said, "Your friend's something." I felt like Nancy was playing all of us.

Gully and Nancy stormed the park, ride after ride after game after game. Luke and I dragged, catching up with them just as they were moving off to the next buzz. I don't know what happened to make us so separate from them, but once I felt it, I couldn't ignore it. And Luke kept looking around, looking worried.

"Is everything okay?" I asked.

He nodded, his face a mask.

"The band that's playing. That's Otis. Remember the guy who sold in the records?" It was on the tip of my tongue to say, "Your sister knew him." It struck me as odd that Luke didn't know about Otis. If Mia had been with him, surely he would have known. Luna Park was a lot of things, but it wasn't the place to ask such questions, even though every minute my mind floated out a new one.

Finally Nancy was tired. We grabbed a booth in the fake tram, and I waved Gully and Luke off to shoot ducks or extract something cheap and flammable by way of the Claw. I pulled a thread out of the stitching of my dress while Nancy filled the water pistol she'd won on the laughing clowns.

"Looks real, doesn't it?"

She pointed it at me and I flinched.

"You're funny." Nancy blew on the tip, then tucked the pistol in her vest pocket. She rearranged her scarf so that it hung long and loose.

"So what's going on with Luke?" she asked.

"We kissed."

"You didn't!"

"We did! In the shop."

"What was it like?"

"It was . . . swift and soft."

Nancy tossed her hair. "Guys who kiss soft are king."

"He's acting weird, though."

"That means he likes you."

"You think?"

"I *know*."

Her phone buzzed. She read the text and put her phone back in her bag. "I want to go on the Scenic Railway, and after that it should be Otis time." I must have looked glum then, because she patted my knee. "It doesn't always have to be just us, you know. It's a big world, monkeyface."

I looked away. Suddenly I felt like I couldn't breathe. There was a fat man sitting on my chest, having a good laugh while he was at it. Nancy noticed my strangled look.

"You okay?"

"No," I spluttered.

"Put your head between your legs. Do it now." She pushed my head down. I took greedy gulps of air. The world smelled rank. After a while my breathing steadied. Slowly I raised my head. I looked out the window. Gully and Luke were standing by the food truck watching the popcorn pop.

"You scared me," Nancy said. She laughed, but I couldn't bring myself to laugh with her.

A REAL GOOD TIME

THE SCENIC RAILWAY WOULD have qualified as an old St. Kildan. It had been around since the 1930s. Its white wood lattice lassoed the park and made all the other rides with their Day-Glo and bad murals look crass. From the highest point I could see St. Kilda's up-down streets, her patches of green, her apartment blocks like computer monitors stacked on top of each other.

"Let's take the first cart," Nancy said. "It'll be scarier."

The man sitting behind us was staring at Nancy. If I could feel it, then she could. He tapped her shoulder and she turned, but only slightly.

"Remember me?" he asked.

"No."

"Come on. You sure you don't remember me?"

Nancy twisted in her seat and took a good long look.

"I don't know you, Jack." She turned back, smiled at me.

But seconds later the guy was at her again. "Why don't you come and sit with me?"

"Because I'm sitting with my girl."

"Are you dykes?"

"Yeah, we're big dykes. We're so dykey it's not funny." Nancy threw her arm around me and went "Mwah" into my neck. I felt a tiny bomb explode inside.

The man leaned forward between us. "How 'bout both of you come sit with me? I'll be piggy in the middle." I could smell his breath. Hot dogs.

The attendant lowered the safety bar, and the man was forced to sit back, but the feeling of menace lingered. Then the cart began to climb and anticipation of another kind fluttered in my stomach. Just before the first big dip he said, "You remember me."

Nancy threw her arms up and screamed.

The cart was clattering, reeling. We jolted with it. Nancy's hair lashed about. Her bangles clashed impressively. She wouldn't grip the bar. My knuckles were white around it. I could see people on the foreshore, the blue sea. Luke and Gully were down at the bottom, over near the carousel with our bags. I waved, but they weren't looking up.

Afterward the attendant lifted the bar, and Nancy and I wobbled down the rickety steps. The guy picked up where he'd left off. On firm ground he was less menacing. His body looked out of proportion. He was short, and he stood like it, stumpy legs spread, chest pushed out. He had a thin mustache and prominent ears. Something about him was familiar—he could have been a customer. He looked like he'd be into Eric Clapton or Rush. Seventies fallout guy.

"Yours," Nancy whispered. Nervous laughter erupted from my mouth.

"What do you say, girls?" His tongue darted skinkishly. "I've got my van. We could have a real good time."

Nancy stopped. She pulled the water pistol from her waistcoat and pointed the pistol at his crotch. "Don't move," she instructed. The man's eyes shot open. He stepped back and put his hands up.

Nancy squeezed the trigger. The man yelped and looked down. It took him a few seconds to realize he wasn't hurt, that the dark patch blooming on the crotch of his jeans was not blood but water. He almost laughed, and then his voice rasped out, "Fuck you, bitch." He grabbed for the pistol and knocked it out of Nancy's hand, and then he got her on the ground, and Nancy—Nancy was amazing. She was like Mickey Rourke or something. I could see tendons popping, lines marking her face. Somehow she ended up straddling him—holding his finger. They were both panting. As she held his finger, Nancy looked at me.

"Don't!" I shouted, because I really thought she was going to do it—break that guy's finger—like the blithe psychopath did to the Hare Krishna—and he was going to die from shock in front of the small crowd that had gathered—but she didn't. She let go, got off him, tossed her hair. The guy stayed on the ground; he looked like he never wanted to get up.

Nancy grinned at me. "I told you it was bullshit."

She stalked off—this beautiful tank—and I hobbled after her, trying to catch up and catch my breath. Somewhere in the back of my mind, pitched way back, the guy's face waited. Where had I seen him before?

I remembered Gully and Luke. We looked where they'd been standing, but they were no longer there. By now the audience was swelling. It was hard to get through them. I felt stricken. I wheeled around, searching for Gully. I heard Nancy's voice above the whirr of panic. "Is that him?"

We started slow and then we were running.

A small crowd surrounded two figures on a bench. Luke and Gully.

Gully sat very still, his feet just hanging in space.

"Gully?" I squeezed his knee. He didn't move.

"What's wrong with him? What happened?"

"I don't know," Luke said. "We were standing where you left us, he said something about the Jeep, and I turned around and he was gone. I looked for him, and when I found him, he was on the ground. I didn't know he was going to run off."

It was only then that I realized I could see Gully's face. No pig snout, just skin, white and vulnerable. Gully stared glassy-eyed at nothing. Nancy had her hand on her hip. She turned to Luke accusingly. "Where were you?"

"I didn't know he'd run off." Luke looked sick. And he was still staring at Nancy like she'd done something to him.

"What?" she snapped.

Luke reached up. His fingers touched the end of her long silver scarf. He tugged and it came off in his hands, and he gripped it.

"How did you get my sister's scarf?" His voice sounded broken.

No one moved. Gully because he was traumatized, me because I was spellbound, Nancy because she was disarmed.

"Give it back," she demanded.

Luke must have seen them all then, like a *Where's Waldo?* of scarf girls. He didn't look at me or Gully or Nancy. He just left, walking fast, merging with the crowd, and he took Nancy's scarf with him.

We had to go to the office and fill out a form. I held Gully's hand. He walked stiffly, hanging his head the way he always did when some unspecified badness had happened at school. In the office a man in a maroon staff shirt asked questions. Did we want to call our father? Did we want to call the police?

"No," I said. "No. Can we just go?"

The man gave Gully a free T-shirt. Nancy steered

us to Acland Street past toxic-tanned girls and money-boys in polo shirts with the collars turned up and European ladies of a certain age, gold chains settling in their creasy necks.

"What about that Luke Casey?" Nancy clicked her tongue. "What a freak!"

I thought about Luke, had flashes of his sad eyes, his dead sister, the card he'd drawn. I saw him standing outside us with his hands in his pockets. I thought of the way he was with Gully: soft, protective. None of this was his fault. I was the one who was supposed to be looking after Gully. Luke didn't know what he was like, not really. I was thinking, hoping, expecting that Nancy would help me face Dad. But when we were two steps shy of the shop, she stopped.

"Aren't you coming in?"

"Sorry, kid." Nancy put her hands on Gully's shoulders. "Courage, Agent Martin. This is just a temporary setback."

She was going back to Otis and the crank of feedback. I watched her go. Part of me wanted to run with her, to fall into step beside her and laugh like Joan Crawford, because my hair was perfect and the world was just a bauble I could carry in a clutch purse. I looked down at Gully, then up at the light from the flat window. Shit. This was not good.

AFTERMATH

DAD WAS IN HIS shorts again, drunkish and dithering around to Fleetwood Mac's *Rumours*. He'd been smiling until he clocked Gully's pale and snoutless face.

He looked at me. "What happened?"

"I don't know."

"Is he—are you all right, champ?"

"He lost his snout."

"Where were you?"

"I was with Nancy on the Scenic Railway. Luke said Gully ran off. I don't know what happened. He won't talk."

Stevie Nicks's warbling was getting out of control. Dad silenced her. He grabbed the phone.

"Who are you calling?" I asked. "We already filled out a form."

"Well, it's not good enough."

Half an hour later we were down at the station with Constable Eve Brennan. Gully wouldn't talk at all. She checked him out for bruises.

"Did someone hurt you?" she asked gently.

Gully gulped and nodded.

"Can you tell me?"

He shook his head slowly. And then he started to heave awful wracking sobs. This went on for a while. I couldn't look at him, so I looked around the room. It was like every police station I'd ever seen on TV. Cubicles and computers. Bulletin boards. Ugly mugs.

Ugly mugs! Recognition flashed white-hot. The guy who had hassled Nancy was one of the Ugly Mugs. I'd seen him on the wall at Streetwise and now again on the cop shop pin board. I stared at his face, his whelk ears and skink tongue, his eyes like tiny tar pits, and felt cold spiking my skin.

"Should I take him to the hospital?" Dad worried in a low voice. "He looks like he's in shock. Gully?"

Gully was shaking his head vehemently.

Dad clutched his keys, but Eve put her hand over his. "I'll take you home," she said. "You've had enough, Bill." She meant drink. Dad didn't argue.

Back at the flat Eve made coffee. She rubbed my arm when she passed me, but all it did was make me feel lonelier. I didn't want her to go, but she did and then it was just me and Dad and the dripping tap in the background, and Gully was in his bed, and there wasn't even *Monkey*.

Dad rubbed his hand through his hair. "I need a drink."

"Don't," I whispered.

He carried the mugs over to the sink. Then he threw them in and snapped.

"You shouldn't have left him alone!"

My voice wobbled all over the place. "We were on the Scenic Railway. It was only ten minutes."

"You don't leave Gully alone."

"I KNOW!"

I ran upstairs. It sounded like the bones of the old building were creaking.

There was a thin strip of light under Gully's bedroom door. I put my ear to the keyhole and heard nothing, no talk, no reportage, no crying, just quiet. In my bedroom I found my box of beautiful people and sifted through them, hoping for inspiration or beauty, something, but nothing came. I stuffed the pictures back in the box and closed the lid. Then I dumped it outside my door.

In my dream Nancy was in the back of the Ugly Mug's van. I was standing in front of it, trying to ignore the rocking. Tourists stopped and stared. I said, "It's not what it looks like," but Nancy was making terrible noises. I tried to open the door. I pulled and pulled on it. I slammed my palms against the tinted windows. "Stop it!" I yelled. "Stop hurting her." But then the door slid open, and Nancy hopped out with blood on her hands. She said, "Yours."

The dream changed to the beach at night: surrealistic sand dunes and waves like wild white horses. Nancy was wearing Gully's snout and running along the shoreline. There was a soundtrack, like a sullen bell clanging, and Nancy was getting farther and farther away until she was just a black dot in the distance.

I didn't know she could run like that.

PART FOUR

Memo #4

Memo from Agent Seagull Martin
Date: Monday, December 15
Agent: Seagull Martin
Address: 34 Blessington St., St. Kilda,
upstairs

POINT THE FIRST:
On December 14 at approximately 2042 two
males accosted the victim outside the Crazy
House at Luna Park.

POINT THE SECOND:
Male 1 pushed the victim to the ground, and
Male 2 yanked off the victim's snout. He
said, "Sorry, little pig-dude," but his face did
not match his words. Male 1 was wearing a
hoodie with a skeleton on it. Both wore jeans
and black sneakers. They ran in the direction
of the Ghost Train, whooping and snorting.

POINT THE THIRD:
Due to the severity of the shove, the victim
did not get a good look at the aggressors. But
his detective's nous tells him the following:
–They were between sixteen and twenty-five.

—They were of similar height and build. Height around five nine. Build: stocky.

POINT THE FOURTH:
Prior to the Snouting, the victim observed at least four instances of young people wearing animal heads/masks.

POINT THE FIFTH:
At the time of the Snouting, "Hold the Line" by Toto could be heard over the PA. This may or may not be significant.

IN SUMMATION
Security at Luna Park is inadequate. The Snouters could well be associated with the Bricker. They share similar sociopathic bent, reckless behavior pattern, and lack of empathy. I suspect they were drug abusers, due to their hyenic laughter, erratic running form, and deployment of the term "little pig-dude."

ACTION
Create identikits to match the attackers' likeness.
Team with SKPD on stopping the rot.

HOLY GRAIL

AFTER THE SNOUTING, GULLY stopped talking. I never knew silence could be so loud or so contagious. Dad was the next to go. He spoke to me only in terse monosyllables and acted like my name had been erased from his lexicon. So I stayed quiet too—what could I say? Gully had been hurt on my watch. The greater dangers of the world—what had once been Gully's spy fodder—had come that little bit closer.

Gully looked different without the snout. He looked younger, more vulnerable. I could see him trying to make his face like a mask. He kept his mouth set like a button and his eyes cast low. It was funny—I never imagined I would miss the snout. I thought about all the times Dad and I had sighed about it. Now it was gone, but we weren't happy. We were breaking apart.

I spent Monday in a fog. At library lunchtime I went through the motions. On Mum's website I typed: *It's all your fault.* But it didn't make me feel any better. Quinn picked up on my mood but didn't press me for an explanation. We stared at our screens, side by side. The world was not hostile, just indifferent, and I saw how it could be—I could drift through it, bumping bodies but never connecting with anyone.

After school Gully was waiting in the usual place. He fell into step beside me. He held his arms straight at his sides, his shoulders squared, and only his hands moved, catching invisible fireflies. I tried faking it.

"Agent Seagull, how was your day?"

Gully's response was to tread faster until he'd overtaken me, and then the sight of his head bent down—minus the snout strap, his schoolbag bouncing on his back, made me feel hopeless and helpless.

When we reached the shop, Gully went straight upstairs. I waited for a moment before pushing open the door. Dad was playing some head-wrecking drone. He was haloed by the record light, his mouth drawn down. He already had a beer cracked. He took a sip and looked at me with solemn, unblinking eyes.

"Where's your brother?"

"He went straight up."

"Has he said anything yet?"

"Nope."

"Right."

That look. I felt so guilty. As if I'd ripped the snout off myself. Dad allowed a puff of air out of his nostrils. The shop sat in quiet disarray. It looked as if he hadn't moved from his stool all day.

"Where's Luke?" I asked.

"He didn't come in."

"Oh." I felt my face heating up and tried to deflect. "Maybe he's sick."

"Well, he picked a great time."

Dad took a long swig from his beer to finish it. He cricked a dent in the can and dropped it below the counter. Then he lumbered off to get a fresh one. I stood still for one, two, three beats; then I lammed and left him to it.

The flat rang with quiet. Sunlight streamed through the window, bouncing off everything and made me feel dizzy. Something was different about the scene. The TV was quiet. Gully was not on the couch; instead he was sitting at the kitchen table. He had found my box of beautiful people and was going through it, scissors in hand, and making little piles of lips and noses and eyes and helmet haircuts.

I tried to meet his eyes. "What are you doing?"

He kept cutting, calmly, silently.

"Talk to me, Gully," I pleaded. "Tell me what's wrong."

I lurked and lingered; I studied the contents of the fridge. "Do you want shish kebabs tonight?"

No response. I slammed the fridge door and rattled out to the living room. I drifted from room to room, feeling melancholy and future homesick. Our building was designed by an Edwardian dwarf; it was all wonky stairs and architraves you could press the flat of your hand upon. Soon all of it would be gone, blasted, the way of the Paradise, replaced with something heartless and architecturally sound.

Gully's bedroom door was open. I pushed it and stepped in. His mess was far worse than mine. His sheets smelled like boy sweat. The floor was a sea of chocolate-bar wrappers and Coke cans, overdue library books on spycraft, and a paper trail of intel in his spiky seismograph handwriting. On the wall Gully had drawn a neat map of St. Kilda, including significant landmarks and a path that marked the Bricker's "Reign of Destruction." He'd identified the shop, the 7-Eleven, Vale and Greeves, Ada's Cakes, and Bernard Levon, Tax Accountant. He'd also noted our stakeout locations for the great white Jeep hunt—each Polaroid was linked to the site with a length of red wool. The end result was like a madman's evidence board. Looking at it made my heart hurt.

I crossed into my room and took in the newly bare walls and Mum's bagged-up tchotchkes. The box from my secret record buy seemed to be announcing itself, so I sat on the floor and started going through it. At the bottom of the pile of records lay a boxed set I hadn't bothered to check at the time—it was opera, and opera didn't sell—but now I juggled the inner case. There in my hands was not the promised seven discs of opera greats but a batch of 45s in their original sleeves. I recognized the labels. They were vintage and they were *nice*; I flipped through the titles, feeling a little pleasure glow. At the last single my fingers froze.

It was "Wishing Well" by the Millionaires, Decca, 1966.

Dad's Holy Grail.

The disk was pristine, so shiny I could practically see my face in it. I carried the record like it was a bomb or a beating heart and placed it gently on my record player. I dropped the needle and held my breath. The song crackled to life, and it was as sweet and deranged as I'd always known it to be. Emotion welled up inside me. It made me feel full and numb at the same time. I fought the urge to run downstairs and present the record to Dad. Only for a second did I allow myself to imagine how his face would transform, how joy would be restored.

You'll see, kids, everything comes in eventually.

But this was a sneaked buy, and now it dawned on me I hadn't even paid for it properly. "Wishing Well" alone was probably worth more than what I'd paid for the whole box. Then again, Rocky hadn't pulled me up on it—was it my fault if he didn't know the value of his own stuff?

The song ended. I played it again. All through dinner and the long hours after, "Wishing Well" stayed in my ear. It felt like the answer to a question I didn't know how to ask, or a present I didn't know how to use.

SKY'S WISHING WELL

QUINN WOULD HELP ME. On the second day of Gully's silence she dumped her bag by my computer and waved her hand in front of my face. My eyes followed five chipped aquamarine nails. "What the hell, Martin? Who died?"

I looked at her face. It was open, waiting, friendly. She looked nothing like a bulldog—how could I have thought that? As the air conditioner groaned above us, I told her about Sunday night. I left out the bit about Nancy and the Ugly Mug. I still wasn't ready to explore that particular patch on my crazy quilt.

"And so now Gully's not talking and Dad blames me, and I blame me, and I don't know if it's going to get better."

Quinn played with her beads. "Does your brother see a psych?"

I shook my head. "He had a behavioral guy for a while, but he's pretty low-maintenance usually."

"All the same. You should get your dad to take him."

"I'm so mad at my dad." My confession sounded puny and plaintive, but Quinn wasn't going anywhere, and then I was able to tell her the rest, about how the amazing Galaxy Strobe had sold us down the river, and Dad hadn't said shit, and the shop was going to hell in a handbasket.

"Maybe he's got a good reason for not telling you," Quinn suggested. "He doesn't know you know, right?"

"Uh-huh."

"Maybe he's too proud."

"Mum says he's in denial."

She nodded slowly. "Maybe you need an independent assessment."

Fast-forward three hours, I presented my dad to Quinn. Or was it the other way around? The shop was quiet. A little tingle told me that Luke hadn't turned up, but I still craned my head, looking for his shadow by the back-room door. Quinn was rocking mechanics overalls and metal dimples. First she asked if he had anything by Throbbing Gristle. Then she told Dad how she could revolutionize his business. "Obviously you need a website. You need a platform. I could help you."

Dad looked at her as if she was speaking Swahili.

As we hustled upstairs, Quinn said, "He's definitely showing signs of disengagement." Gully was at the kitchen table again. Quinn and I circled him, checking out his work. He'd arranged the lips and ears and eyes and haircuts and was busy pasting them onto pieces of paper, making composite faces.

I finally caught on. "Identikits!" I cried.

Quinn and I waited as the silence grew. I felt my mood plummet. Gully looked up at me. I crouched by his ear. "Gully, if you don't start talking soon, Dad's never going to forgive me." He shifted slightly in his seat. Not a smile, not a look, not a crumb. "I'll leave you to it," I said grimly, turning on my heel and marching upstairs with Quinn cool in my wake.

Quinn gave my bedroom the same forensic eye that I had given hers. She considered blankness, the row of packed suitcases. Her foot nudged a bin-bag. "What's all this?"

"Mum's stuff. I used to have it up everywhere."

"I get it. You think if you hang on to her stuff, she might come back to claim it one day. I did the same thing with my dad. Only he didn't have so much. I found this T-shirt of his and wore it till it was all gross and holey." She bent down to pick up the Noddy eggcup. "You should have a clearing. You can't have your mum's energy muscling in all the time—you'll get lost."

"I could take it all to the thrift shop."

Quinn smacked my arm lightly. "Don't give it away. Sell it at Fat Helen's or put it on Goldmine or something."

"My life for sale."

"Not your life. Hers." Quinn's eyes roved the bags. Her voice went soft. "After Mum and Dad split, I didn't see him for ages. I thought he was living in Queensland,

and then one day I ran into him at Fed Square with his new wife and he had, like, a three-year-old, and Mum hadn't told me. I had coffee with him and his wife and child. It was the worst hour of my life. Grown-ups are just like kids but bigger. They're scared of us because they think we'll catch them out, burst their bubbles." She poked the air and made a popping sound. "After that I decided I was always going to be straight up. If I didn't like a person, I wasn't going to pretend. I don't ever want to be a faker." She patted her camera, slung around her neck. "That's why I don't do digital."

I smiled. Quinn was analog. "You're one of us, then."

"What I've been trying to tell you. Now show me the single."

I played her "Wishing Well." Quinn nodded along to the dorky beat. Then she pulled out her laptop, and we checked out how much Rocky's records were really worth.

"You want to list them?" Quinn asked.

"Don't I need a credit card?"

"You can use mine."

"Really?"

"As long as you don't go charging up hotels and bitches." She laughed. "And I want a cut—ten percent."

"Deal! Okay!" I started to arrange the records in alphabetical order for no reason other than it made me feel slightly more in control. "Dad won't let us have a computer at home. He thinks I'm going to hook up with a cannibal or something."

"It's a legitimate concern," Quinn conceded.

After that it was easy. Credit card in, address, etc. I had to create a profile—I called my "shop" *Sky's Wishing Well* and even borrowed Dad's tagline. *Nothing over 1995.*

It took us a little over an hour to list the records. I was careful to note the condition but couldn't help adding enthusiastic sidenotes and smileys. In the lull that followed with the laptop still warm, we returned to our regular haunts: Quinn to Otisworld, me to Galaxy Strobe. There was a link to her video installation, "My Blizzard."

"Play it," Quinn urged, so I did.

What can you say about your mother in darkness, wearing an outfit fringed with seventy thousand tampons? When she go-go dances with her face set like a tragedy mask, and the whirl of white threatens to blind you?

Quinn looked a little wistful. "I can't help it. I still think she's awesome. I can separate the art from the person."

I pointed to the bags. "If you see anything you want in there, you can have it."

They don't teach you how to make friends at school. How one day, if it's the right person, you can open up and empty out, and then they can pour their story into your space, and this shifting of components goes on until you're mixed good. Quinn left with a big portion of Mum's stuff, and she was right about that, too—I did feel clearer. I felt almost hopeful, like I had done something toward improving our lot. The only problem was as soon as I left my bedroom, the positive ions slid into reverse. The silent Martin males were excellent vibe killers. They skulked and sulked; they kept their eyes averted. I couldn't stand to be around them. I made a desultory dinner of sausages and mash and then raced back to the safety bedroom, where I played the saddest songs in the world. All my maudlin boys: Nick Drake and Jackson C. Frank and Tim Hardin. I played "It'll Never Happen Again" three times in a row. The mournful piano was like a finger prodding me, like Gully's voice, back when he used to use it: Sky, Sky, Sky, Sky.

A DARE AND A DREAM

O N WEDNESDAY MORNING THE postie dropped off an express post parcel from Japan: Gully's Christmas present wrapped in delicate rice paper. Dad tried to use it for leverage. He held the brick in front of Gully. "You can open it early if you say something." Gully kept his mouth fixed firm. "What the hell," Dad said, his lips twisting with hurt. "You can open it anyway."

Night vision goggles. *With head mount to leave hands free for manipulation.* Whatever that meant. I knew Gully was excited; he had to be. But his face stayed stiff as concrete as he placed the contraption over his head and adjusted the straps and milked the LED lights. He promptly set off for the darkest room in the house, the under-stairs cupboard, and only came out when Dad threatened to break the door down. Following that, he was strangely compliant. Dad secured a silent promise that Gully would take the goggles off as soon as he got to school.

"I've got a bad feeling about this," Dad groaned. "He's gonna get arrested."

"They have to catch him first," I said.

I walked up Carlisle Street with my weirdo brother, and I tried to deflect all the rubberneckers. He had the goggles on the head mount. I could see his face below. There was the tiniest hint of a smile, but he still looked like a baby sniper.

It was our second-to-last day of term. Without the seniors, school looked like a ghost town. My class sat slack and starey. Even the teachers had given up on the idea that we were there for any reason other than cheap child care. I spent the morning thinking about Luke Casey—specifically his absence from the shop. I had a feeling about it. He wasn't sick; he was hiding out. Five minutes into a DVD about a Mennonite community, I walked out of class and off the school grounds.

Out in the world the sky looked dramatic. It had rained overnight and the streets smelled like burned toast. The sun was bright and the scattered clouds had dark edges. I caught the tram down to the junction and then to the beach. The marina glittered in the distance; her mess of masts looked like a giant's game of pick-up sticks. Soon I was at the fence watching the boats clank and bob. The marina was always in development; there had been attempts to turn it into a commercial hub, with cafés and boat sales and even a classy restaurant, but in true St. Kilda style, the old vibe still clung. The marina was home to movement, not all of it visible. There were faces behind shutters, crusty fisherman types, businessman-dreamers. They didn't care about cafés. They loved the water because the water was always there. Like god or something.

The main gate was open. In a beige cubicle above the sales showroom a woman sat behind an information desk. She waited for me to speak. I spoke like I was Gully.

"I'm looking for Luke Casey."

"He'll be down around the dry docks."

I waited, clearly needing translation. She jerked her head toward the window. "Down there. On your right. Big shed stacked with boats. You can't miss it."

But I still couldn't seem to move. I felt suddenly flooded with nervousness. What if Luke didn't want to see me?

The woman peered at me. "Okay, love? You've gone green."

"I'm fine," I squeaked before running down the stairs.

Two black swans by the dry dock sheds; a bright blue sky behind them. I found Luke straightaway. He was cleaning a boat. He had his shirt off. Which was both nice and unnerving. The only other nude chests I'd seen belonged to Dad and Gully and uninhibited backpackers. He turned around and caught me gaping. He scrunched the rag in his hand and smiled a slow, sure smile. My nervous feeling dissipated.

"Hi," I said.

"Hi."

We stared at each other. Centuries passed. Luke went back to cleaning.

"How's Gully?"

"Hmm. He's not talking. He hasn't said one word since the Snouting. He sent us a memo, so we know what happened. Two guys knocked him down, and one of them took the snout. I don't think it was personal, but you know Gully."

Luke put his rag down. "Yeah."

We both started to speak at once. We hung our heads, made motions toward laughter.

"You go," I said.

Luke smiled. "No, you."

My words came out in a rush. "It wasn't your fault. You couldn't have known he'd run off. What Nancy said—I should have said something back, but there was too much happening. . . . Is that why you haven't been in the shop?"

Luke didn't say yes or no. "I've been thinking it's time I went home. If I get my shit together, I can go to uni next year. Make my mum smile."

"Oh." I studied an oil stain on the floor.

"I'm not really record shop material."

"I don't know about that," I lied. "You could at least stay until Christmas. I—I like you there."

"You do?"

I met his eyes. "Yeah. I do."

Luke found his T-shirt and stretched it over his

head. His voice came out muffled through the material. "Do you want a cup of tea?"

Around me boats bobbed and gulls hovered. "Where?"

He took my hand and led me around the back of the docks. We went through a small door into a large shed. Sunlight streamed through tiny holes in the tin and made the walls look starry. The space was filled with boat business: paddles, ropes, life jackets. The smell of methylated spirits hung in the air; also, faintly, potato chips. In one corner there was a camp bed and stove; in another a work table with some screens and tins of paint and emulsion.

"This is where you sleep?"

Luke nodded.

"What do you do for a bathroom?"

"There's a bathroom." He smiled. "Why—do you need it?"

"No!"

Luke hunkered by the stove. I heard the hiss and catch of gas and flame. I moved around, looking at things. On top of the worktable there were screens of Mia's face in reverse.

"Who owns this place?"

"A guy I met. I do some work around here, painting and cleaning, some repairs, and he lets me stay."

Luke stirred sweetened condensed milk into my tea and passed it to me. It was sickly sweet, too hot to drink. I felt hot all over, prickly. He sat on his bed and looked up at me. I paused before sitting next to him. The camp bed creaked and then quiet descended. He reached across me and I felt suddenly conscious that he was making a move, but when he brought his hand back, Nancy's scarf was in it. He gave it to me. I wrapped it around my hand. The fabric felt silky cool.

"Can I trust you?" Luke asked. I nodded, my throat too tight to talk.

He gave me a photo. The photo was of Mia. The angle suggested she had taken it herself. She looked ecstatic, her eyes caught somewhere between a dare and a dream. And she was wearing a silver scarf.

"That was in her stuff too," Luke said. "I got a shock when I saw your friend with the same scarf. Well, I've seen a few more since."

"The Girlfriends of Otis."

"I guess Mia was with him or into him."

I thought about the photo on Otisworld, what Quinn had said about there being girls like Mia, only Mia had it worse. I tried to think of a way to tell him that wouldn't sound seedy, and then I lost my nerve. I stared at the photo. The background looked familiar—an old wardrobe with a gilt handle—but I couldn't place it.

"I just want to talk to him," Luke went on. "I mean, Otis. Like, if I talked to him, maybe he could tell me something good about her." Luke's fingers were grazing mine. He said, "I went into your dad's shop because of the tape. I was trying to talk to him about it and he offered me a job. So then it felt like fate, which would be okay if I believed in fate."

"I believe in it," I said. I became aware of how close he was, how my school dress was sticking to my back with sweat. Luke took his glasses off, rubbed his eyes. He looked at me. In that second I knew he was going to kiss me, and I knew I was going to let him. His hand curved around my waist while his knee knocked a stack of books, and then he was bracing my body with his. The camp bed creaked beneath us.

Time is a funny thing. It's slippery when you want it and frozen when you don't. And sometimes it's like it doesn't exist at all. From Nancy's stories I never got that you could kiss someone and make time disappear; that you could press against them and when you finally came apart, you felt like a changed person.

When the kissing stopped, Luke's face was fond and a little rueful. He touched my hair, my cheek, my lips. I shivered. Nancy had never said anything about feelings, either. She talked in concrete terms. A guy was hot. He made her feel lush. She never said how her head felt. Mine felt crazy; it was as if my world had shrunk and Luke filled the frame. It was too fast and it made me nervous.

I got up and smoothed myself out.

"I'd better lam, I mean, I better go . . ." I blinked and back-stepped and leaned against the door smiling, and I bet my smile looked like a maniac's smile. I fumbled behind my back for the handle and then opened the door and ran out of the shed. The sun nearly killed me with its sudden brilliance—a thousand flashcubes popping at once. I headed for the beach. *How do you feel?* I ran along the sand, taking great gull strides as though I could outpace my heart. *Happy!* My body ringing like a bell. *Happy! Happy!*

BABY ELEPHANT TRAUMA

I WAS A DAZED girl walking past kids on skateboards and little old ladies with matching pugs. I didn't have a plan, or even a destination. It was as if my brain had switched off and it was muscle memory sending me south, back to the gray bridge where the garden was crowded with vistas of blooming marigolds. I ventured down to the Purple Onion, looking for Nancy, but I couldn't see her, just a sourpuss waitress with a bad bouffant. She kept her eye on me as she moved around the tables, and finally came right up.

"Can I help you?"

"Is Nancy working?"

"Who?"

"Nancy Cole."

The waitress blinked at me. I looked into her blank eyes. Nope. Nothing was connecting. I started trying to describe Nancy but then remembered I had a photo of her on my phone. I flashed the photo, and the waitress shifted her feet. Her new posture was aggressive, her lips drawn in a smirk.

"You mean Lisa. She's gone. She got sacked. Stealing. Ages ago."

"Oh." I froze for a moment. I craned my head past her to squiz inside the dome. The bald, tattooed chef glared up from whatever he was chopping. He looked like he should have been cooking crank, not scrambled tofu. The waitress huffed. "Anything else?"

I shook my head.

"Does she owe you money?"

I shook my head again.

"Well, tell her if she shows her face back here, Milo's going to rearrange it."

I'll tell you a secret. Nancy's not my real name.

One night, not so long ago, Nancy had danced in front of my mirror in a 1960s cocktail dress. Connie Francis was singing "Where the Boys Are," and Nancy stopped swaying to say, "Did you know that sharks have to move forward or they die? It's a fact." She started swaying again. She made her hand into a fin and weaved it through invisible waves. She kept talking, in that way she had, that always made me feel like I was about to lose my footing. "Like me," she said. "Always moving forward."

We were foggy from Dunlops. I was swaying too.

"Consider this: elephants have to be happy or they die. But they have long memories, so if they suffered some baby elephant trauma—like hunters killed their mama—they never, ever, ever get over it. . . ."

Nancy sat down eventually. She dropped flat on her

back and stared up at the crack in my ceiling.

"Your crack's getting bigger." Her sad half smile.

I lay next to her and imagined the ceiling tumbling down raining chunks of plaster until all that was left was me and Nancy on the bed, like some Grecian ruin, so beautiful and so damaged.

A storm was brewing. The sky had gone technicolor. The sun burned. Heat was rising up from the cement. I took out my phone and didn't even try to be creative.

Where are you? And, seconds later, *Who's Lisa?*

CRACKING UP

GULLY WASN'T WAITING AT the gate. I nabbed a kid from his class, held him by the bag strap. "Where's Gully?"

"Your dad had to come and get him."

"What did he do?"

"He wouldn't take the goggles off."

The kid smirked. I felt a flash of rage. "Don't smile, you little shit." The boy's face slid. He broke away from me and ran.

When I got to the shop, the CLOSED sign was facing out. I pressed my head against the glass for several seconds, but I couldn't see Dad in there. I started to feel hot, knotty. I raced up the stairs to the flat, where the silence greeted me like a smack in the face. I searched the kitchen for clues and couldn't find any. What to do? I tried sitting, but it only made me more anxious. I flubbed around, tidied. I turned the TV on and then off again. I opened and closed the fridge door. I worked away at ancient Blu Tack stains. I thought about playing some records, but it seemed wrong somehow. The phone rang and I jumped. It was a telemarketer. I hung on to the receiver and thought about ringing Eve, but something stopped me.

By eight o'clock I had sunk into numbness. I was sitting now, and the TV was on, but the sound was turned down. I knew it was irrational, but I was worried that they'd left me. That was why when I heard the key in the door and saw Dad emerge from the shadows of the stairs, my first instinct was to hug him. It was like hugging a statue. I pulled back. His face was gray and his expression was one of weary distaste. Gully was behind him, still in the night vision goggles, LED lights winking. He went straight to his bedroom, and Dad went straight to the Dunlops. He took a long drink and then leaned against the fridge. "We went to see Ross," he said.

Ross was Gully's last best behavioral therapist.

"What did he say?"

"He wants us to come back tomorrow."

I nodded. "Okay. Dad—" I was ready to talk about the shop. *We're going to be all right,* I'd say. *I can feel it in my waters.* But suddenly he snapped. "If you'd been looking after your brother like you were supposed to, we wouldn't be here now, like this."

My eyes felt hot. "That's not fair!"

"Jesus, I thought we were at the end of it," Dad said. "Everything we do, all the walking on eggshells and the positive reinforcement and sticking to routine, it's all bullshit! He's gone backward." Dad pushed himself off the fridge door and carried his beer out to the living room. I crashed around the kitchen; I started cooking and cleaning as if that would help. Gully's identikits reproached me from the kitchen table. The composite faces made me want to cry. They didn't look like anyone.

We made it through dinner. Gully silent. Dad drinking solidly. The sound of his slurping drove me crazy. Then afterward, the room was too hot. *Monkey* was too loud. Dad rolled a cigarette. He twisted the end and put it in his mouth and looked at me, like there were questions he wanted to ask but he didn't speak my language. I watched the smoke unfurl in a cloud around his head.

"Why don't you have any friends your own age?"

"I don't know. Because I'm weird, Dad. Because you're weird. *We're* weird. It has to come from somewhere. Because Mum makes video art wearing tampons. Because we live here and you don't stock CDs and you talk about Lou Reed and Bob Dylan like they're close personal friends, and it's the twenty-first century and don't you even know that smoking causes lung cancer!" I grabbed the cigarette from his mouth and pitched it in the sink and then stormed up to my bedroom.

While Janis Joplin screeched and howled, I changed out of my uniform. I put on a dress, blue for my mood. I tugged on furry brown Rasputin boots, the bead necklace, and Luke's wristband. I packed my phone, my wallet. I swiped my mouth with Mum's red lipstick and then I was ready.

Dad was waiting on the landing. "Where do you think you're going?"

"Out."

"I don't think so."

Dad's face wobbled. I thought he was about to crack a smile, but no, he was just about to crack. Full stop. I tried to walk past him, but he grabbed my arm.

"You're staying here. I want you at home. You've got responsibilities."

And then *I* cracked. I opened my mouth and let my insides out.

"Why is Gully my responsibility? He's your son! If you want to shout at someone, shout at Mum. She's the one who left because it was all so hard."

Dad slapped my cheek. No one saw *that* coming. It stung and I pressed my hand there. I felt a loud whirring—my brain on spin cycle—Dad's mouth moving in apology, but I couldn't even hear him. Then he was staring at his hand like it didn't belong to him. Then at me, and Gully was in the doorway staring at me too.

"Item." My voice was clear and loud. "Mum sold the shop."

Gully stared from me to Dad.

"Sky—" Dad started, but I tore through him.

"Mum rang me and she told me. She's sold the shop. Boom!" It felt weirdly satisfying to throw Dad's words back at him, but only for a second, and then we were staring, straight-lipped, at each other. Inside I was falling apart. "You knew." My voice shook a little. "You knew and you didn't say a *fucking* word."

Gully's chin began to tremble. He opened his mouth, and a high-pitched wail came out.

I bolted.

"Sky!" Dad called after me. "I'm sorry, love."

But it was too late. I was down the steps and out the door, where the warm night air almost felt like forgiveness.

MUGS AND MARKS

I WALKED FAST AND didn't stop until my feet were scuffing the grass outside Nancy's. Ray's brown brick cottage sat at the lagging end of the canal, where the water thinned out to a brown trickle, and the sides were crowded with good times had: dead cigarettes and six-pack rings, condoms and potato chip packets. A hundred years ago the area was swampland. The air was sulfurous, and even the ducks looked like they wanted to be somewhere else. I knocked on the door. Ray opened it. I got a blast of leeks. He was in his kimono. I didn't look up or down. I stared somewhere over his dandruffy shoulder.

"She's in her room." He called out, "Nancy? Your little friend is here."

Ray waddled ahead of me, clearing a path through the stacks of books. Books everywhere! Books on fencing and how to knit jumpers out of cat fur; books on theosophy and the myriad ways to tie a scarf; books on tantric sex and better gun maintenance. They were dusty, smelly, unsorted—I didn't want to think about the state of Ray's psyche.

Nancy was bobbing around to some surf instru-
mental, dressed in a black slip and bare skin. She had
a hundred silver bracelets up and down her arms, and
her hair looked like thrown flames. I waited until she
noticed me, and then she surprised me with the force of
her embrace. She crushed her chest against mine, and
wheezed. "Dollbaby!" She hit me with kisses. I could
smell whiskey on her breath. Then she assessed me at
arm's length.

"Cute dress. What gives?"

"I had a fight with Dad." I took a breath and thrust
my chin forward. "He slapped me, so I walked out."

"Jesus. Bill slapped you? Bill?"

The way she was looking at me made my cheek hurt
all over again.

"Was he pissed?"

I sank onto her bed, and then I couldn't help crying.
I guess I was in shock, and now it all came out. Nancy
sat next to me. She rubbed my shoulders. She did it
brusquely like I was in the corner and she wanted me
back in the ring, and then she moved off and went back
to the mirror. She picked up her eyeliner and drew
sweeping lines, the perfect cat eyes.

"How's Gully?"

"He's not talking. He hasn't said a word for four
days."

"What's in the water, kid?"

"I don't know."

She turned from the mirror and reached for a joint in the ashtray. She lit it and toked and passed it along. I dragged deeply, had to bury my cough in her pillow.

"Can I stay here?"

"Bad timing. I've got someplace to be."

"Can I come?"

She shook her head.

"Is it a date or an assignation?"

Nancy's eyebrows went up, and she allowed a small laugh.

"It's a party." She seemed to be looking at me from a different angle and reassessing the situation. "It's a very grown-up party."

I rolled my eyes, faked insouciance. "What are we talking? Plushies, hot tubs, swinging suburbans?"

Nancy laughed her donkey-honk laugh. Then she sorted out her hair, and I stared at the collage on her cupboard door. It was like a map of her desires: cave houses, Greek islands, wild-looking artists, and femme fatales. One picture showed a tattooed man; he was so inked I could hardly see his face.

"Jack Dracula," Nancy said. "I always used to wonder what he looked like naked. I used to imagine I was his girlfriend. We'd fuck and then he'd tell me the story of each tattoo."

Nancy saying "fuck" like that—as a verb—suddenly made me dizzy. When she said it, I saw it. I saw it so

clearly I had to work to lose the image of Nancy and
Jack Dracula going at it. My eyes raced around the
cupboard. I took in the chips in the wood, the ornate
handle. I fixed on a photo of a girl in a communion
dress, flanked by smiling parents.

"Is that you?"

"In another life."

I became conscious of the music then. It was the
bent, kerplunky intro to "Wishing Well."

"That's so weird," I said.

"What's so weird?"

"That song. It's the Millionaires."

I started to explain the significance, Dad and his
Holy Grail, the single that Rocky had sold in, but Nancy
had already tuned out.

"A guy gave it to me. You know what it means when
a guy gives you a mix tape? True Fucking Love."

"Was it Otis?"

"No comment."

Nancy disappeared into the hall. I prowled around
her room. My hands floated over tampons, Nag Champa
incense, orphan earrings. I bent down and got level
with the tape player, watched the spindles turn. The
tape in there was one of ours—I could tell by the little
wishing well. There was no writing on the label, but it
bore the same mark as the tape that Luke had shown
me, Mia's tape.

The Millionaires ended and a raga swirled up.

Nancy came back with her hair in a cloud around her head. She made a face, pushed stop. "I hate that hippie shit. Come on, dollbaby. Let's blow."

We walked along the canal. Nancy walked a four-four beat. The click of her heels on the cement made me feel like we were in a movie. Around us the sky was turning dark corduroy-blue. Pigeons were returning to their palm tree caves. Gnats hovered above the water, which moved slow and shiny-thick as an oil slick. Suddenly, Nancy stopped. She turned slightly to face the wall. There, on the bricks, was a poster of Mia. This one had writing on it, though; someone had drawn a flower crown, the letters *RIP* curled among the flowers. Poking in the holes in the brickwork were candles of different colors and lengths; it was a shrine to match my own. It made me feel seasick.

Nancy produced a hip flask from her bag and took a sip. "This is where they found her," she said somberly.

"How do you know?"

"Ray told me." She seemed to be on the verge of saying more. She stayed there, silent. Then she toasted Mia's image and passed me the flask. I sipped. Nancy took her lighter out and lit the candles, and I let the flickering light lull me. I pictured Mia in her silver dress weaving along the road. Cars honking, her giving them the finger. I saw her standing over the canal seeking her reflection in the water. And then . . . did she just fall in? Did she cry out at the shock of the cold?

"Dollbaby," Nancy said.

The light from the candles danced on the water. I thought I saw something moving down there. I pictured Mia rising, ghostly and calm, but it was just an old beer can bobbing up.

Nancy reeled me back. "Otis asked me to go to America with him."

"You don't sound very excited."

"It's better if I do my own thing."

"I think you're right."

She started laughing. She didn't stop for ages.

"What?" I said.

"You don't know anything about it."

Was she being mean? I couldn't tell. It sounded like she was. Was she mad at Otis or mad at me? I stared at the poster—Mia's dark, unknowable eyes. The Ugly Mug rose up then. I had pushed him away, but he wouldn't stay down.

"Nancy."

"Sky."

"Who was that guy from the Scenic Railway?"

"What guy?"

"You know."

Nancy stopped. She shook her head. Then she started walking again, a little faster now. "Okay. I'll tell you. He's a mark."

"A what?"

"A mark. A guy a girl can put the squeeze on."

I didn't get it.

Nancy tutted. "I only went with him once. Don't judge."

"What did you do?"

"*I* didn't do anything. He did it all himself. Then he called me a slut and gave me twenty dollars." She looked at me sideways. "He knows Ray. That's how it happened. Sometimes, to pay the rent, I do Ray a favor." She stopped again. "I shouldn't have told you. You're shocked. Look. It's not emotional. It's not even me—it's like . . . You want to know who Lisa is? Well, now you know. She's my alter ego. Every girl should have one. You let her do the stuff the real you wouldn't think about."

"It's ugly," I blurted.

"Yeah, well."

"Is that what tonight is?"

In the shadows Nancy's mouth looked like a cut in her face.

"Go home, little sister."

I couldn't help following her, though. Even as she stepped faster, and shook me away with the backs of her hands. Across the highway, along the beach toward the marina—Nancy had stopped acknowledging me, but still I followed her. I was lagging behind, or she was moving faster. When she reached the gate, she turned and gave me a blank smile and slipped through. Some of the boats were lit up but not all. I took my shoes off and left them on a bench and trod soundlessly behind her. Water moved beneath the wood and slapped against hulls. It was warm out, but I was shivering. Nancy burled up to a white yacht. It had "ZAZEN" scrawled on the side in Japanese-y font. I felt disappointed. Why hadn't she just said she was meeting Otis? She marched up the steps and rapped on the door. The door opened— all I saw was a dark triangle—and in she went. After a while the light in the yacht went out. I stared at the dark space for a few seconds more before making my way back to my shoes.

I could have gone home. It wasn't much after ten. But the joint had made my mind expansive. People. The World. We were all such liars. We didn't want what was right in front of us; we wanted other realities. Gully wanted to be cracking codes and collaring bad guys. Nancy wanted to be a heartbreaker with a mink stole and a smoking gun. Dad wanted to go back to when he could drink without a hangover and his only responsibility was to himself. Luke wanted to go back too, to do it all again, only better. And what about me? What did I want? Skylark Martin, resident bird. I knew Mum's shadow loomed large. I looked for her in everyone.

Nancy's collage floated through my mind. The array of pictures presented themselves as on the walls of a gallery. The real Nancy dwelled somewhere between

Jack Dracula and the girl in the communion dress, but I would never know her.

And then something clicked. Nancy's collage, Nancy's cupboard. Suddenly I knew why it looked so familiar. The gilt handle was the same gilt handle behind Mia Casey in her ecstatic self-portrait.

Nancy had a tape. Mia had a tape.

Nancy stayed at Ray's. Mia stayed at Ray's.

Nancy had never told me how she'd ended up as Ray's flatmate, and I'd never asked. But it seemed to me a certain type of man would always find a certain type of girl. Before Nancy there was Mia; before Mia there was probably some other lost girl.

Ray collected books and fallen robins. He put the former on a blanket and the latter on the job. The world turned on need and gratification, want and get, and if we weren't working one, we were wrangling the other.

I could have gone home, but I didn't. I went to see Luke.

MIDNIGHT CONFESSIONS

I KNOCKED ON THE tin door, and the echo bounced around, almost scaring me into retreat. Luke opened the door, wearing shorts and a look of rumpled contentment that quickly turned to surprise.

"Were you asleep?" I asked, pushing past him, Nancy-style.

"No, just reading. Where have you been?"

"Everywhere." I headed straight for the camp bed. His sleeping bag was open. I climbed into it. He hesitated and then squeezed in next to me. It was the loveliest shock to feel his limbs against mine. We lay Siamese-ly staring up at the shadows of moths.

I could hear the waves rolling and the jar-and-clank marina music. After a while I started to talk, and then it was like I couldn't stop. I told him about the mix tapes with the matching symbols, about Otisworld and the website. I told him how Ray had said Mia was a party girl, but Granny didn't know her and that Nancy did stuff with guys for money and maybe Mia had too. Luke let me talk. He took it all in and when I finished, we were both quiet for a long time. Luke sat up. He put his head in his hands. I watched his shoulders moving up and down, but I didn't try to touch him. His voice sounded warm and scratchy, like old vinyl. He said, "I came here because I wanted to say good-bye to Mia, but it feels like she won't let me."

"She's still here," I said. "I can feel her." I leaned my head into his back and felt the vibrations of his breathing. "I hate good-byes."

Luke turned around. His lips met mine and time did its slow elapse. My last thought before drifting off to sleep was that I needed to get home. A few hours later I awoke with Luke's arm under my neck. The light in the room was eerie. I tasted the sea in the air. The seagulls started early, their cries catapulting me up to a sitting position.

"Luke!" I shook his shoulder.

He smiled at me sleepily.

"I have to get home." I hauled myself out and rearranged my clothes. Luke's arms went for my waist. He tried to wrest me back to the camp bed. I fell against him, allowed myself the sweet reprieve.

Luke sat up and sighed. "Do you have to go?" Then he reached for his shoes. "I'll take you."

The sunrise came up fierce and pink. Outside the shop Luke took my arm.

"I dreamed about her," he said. "That never happened before."

I thought of my dreams of Mia and was almost too

scared to ask, "Was it a good dream?" Luke nodded. Above our heads the living room was illuminated. I saw shadows through the curtains. I kissed Luke good-bye, took a breath, and went for the door.

"Sky, Sky, Sky, Sky, Sky, Sky, Sky!"

Gully rushed me, clamping onto my waist, giving my heart a power surge.

"Where did you go? We thought you'd gone forever."

Gully's voice went right through me. Eve was getting up from the couch, smoothing her hands on her jeans. She gave me a tentative smile, her face dimpled with concern. Dad appeared in the kitchen doorway, a mug in his hand. I lifted my eyes to meet his. He put his mug down and came toward me, a thousand sorrows etched across his old man face. He hugged me and made a small fretful croak against my hair.

"I'm so, so sorry," he said. He pulled back to look at me. "Are you okay?"

I nodded. I couldn't look at him; tears were building behind my eyes.

"I've just been so . . . worried," Dad said. "I should have told you about the shop. I'm sorry. And I never should have hit you." He started crying then. It was awful seeing his face contort, his mouth opening like a trapdoor and his eyes racing as his face reddened. My tears gushed forth. Gully stared at us. "It's official," he said, in his most official voice. "I'm upset." Waterworks all around.

"I don't want to move to the country," I spluttered.

Dad wiped his eyes and blew his nose. "Who said anything about moving to the country?"

"I thought we were going to Aunty V's."

"No."

"Well, where are we going, then?"

"Your mum's folks are in assisted living now, so we can stay in their place for a while. If . . ." He cast a quick eye on Gully. "If you want to. There's still the beach. Really, it's like an inverted St. Kilda. Or like St. Kilda before all the yuppies got their claws in. It could be okay."

Newport. The concrete flamingos. The fantasia lamp. The stockpile of perishables. The little notes on everything.

Eve moved next to me on the couch. She put her arm around me. It felt good. "Old St. Kildans never die. They just cross the water."

Morning streamed in the window, throwing a starchy light on everything.

"What about the shop?" My question hung in the air with the dust motes. Gully was skywriting again, big and looping letters. He started to hum.

Dad coughed. "We may have to diversify." He paused. "Is that what all this is about?"

I rolled my eyes, faking cool. "I'm just rebelling, Dad."

"You think you can give it a rest until after Christmas?"

"I can if you can."

Gully peered up at Dad. "Do I have to go to school today?"

"What do you want to do?"

"Work in the shop."

Dad looked at me. "Skylark?"

I grinned. School or shop? There was no contest.

Dad made a cage over Gully's face with his hands. Gully chortled. Eve stroked my hair gently the way Galaxy Strobe never had. I leaned in and surrendered to the warm. For the tiniest moment my mind allowed the future in. It looked doable.

THE END OF VINYL

D ATE: THURSDAY, DECEMBER SEVENTEENTH. Time: 1000 hours. Location: Wishing Well Operation. Grand Sale." Gully lowered his fist and beamed. He was ready for action: tool belt primed, night vision goggles in hands-free mode.

"Where do you want me?"

Dad turned Captain Beefheart down a smidge.

"Skylark, Seagull, I want everything out. I mean, everything. Let's bung some crates on the footpath and start making capital. Sky, I want you to pull whatever's been in the racks for more than six months and mark it down by half. Gully, I need you to make a sign for the front window. When you've done that, you can start shifting the g-sale stock out to the street. Now, where the hell is Luke?"

I'd been wondering the same thing. Every time I thought about him, I felt a little thrill in the pit of my stomach. When he walked in at ten thirty and smiled straight at me, it was like I was steeped in blush.

"What's the matter with you?" Gully put his palm to my forehead. I brushed him aside and got busy. The last thing I needed was my crush splashed all over Gully's next memo.

I felt okay about culling but not so happy about the markdowns. We had good stock; our problem was exposure, or lack of it. I thought about Goldmine: the records I'd listed with Quinn. Possible future listings sat everywhere I looked.

Weeding out dead stock. I started at the *As*—Luke started at the *Zs*—we were going to meet in the middle, and we were inching closer and closer. When we got there, I would stop time and kiss him. I imagined our hearts booming out of our skins like those old animations. The morning turned on tiny moments: furtive grins and sneaky hands. Captain Beefheart was loud enough to hide our crushing, but it was only a matter of time before Dad and Gully got wise.

GRAND SALE—THE END OF VINYL.

Gully held up his sign and waited for the verdict.

"Nice," I said.

Dad bowed his head. "Prophetic."

"Not necessarily," I started to say, then thought better of it. I would tell him about Goldmine—I just had to wait until he'd calmed down. Dad was sorting, humming—you could see where Gully got it from. I hadn't seen this kind of energy for years. His blood was up, no doubt. I hung back and enjoyed it from a distance.

On this last Thursday before Christmas we were an industrious bunch. Dad put out new stock while Luke and I picked over the old. By lunchtime the racks were looking positively roomy. Eve showed up and Dad nicked off. Gully parked himself out front next to the sale table. So for the next little bit it was just Luke and me, and it was lovely. He gripped my hands below the counter and pressed his knees against mine. "How's it going?"

"Good." I smiled. Luke checked to see that Gully was beyond visual range, and then he kissed me, fast.

He drummed his foot on the carpet. "I can't concentrate."

"Me neither."

A customer in Soundtracks muttered, "Get a room."

Gully came in complaining of the heat, so I put him to work refilling the racks. He trawled slowly, pausing to read liner notes or inspect the discs for secret messages in the runoff. His slowness was calming. I needed to feel calmer.

And then: "Hellooo." Steve Sharp strolled toward us rock star–ishly—I guess you never lose it. I marveled again at his tight skin, his impossible teeth so straight and white they looked like a mouthguard.

"Where's the boss?"

"Out."

He nodded and looked around the shop. He seemed to be assessing it, and then I felt ill. Urban Renewal. Mum had sold to Steve Sharp, the Buddhist property developer. He was going to turn the Wishing Well into loft apartments. In twenty years St. Kilda would just be a grid of posh boxes and dry gardens, and her people would be wax-perfect and soulless. Steve Sharp kept gazing around, his lips pursed.

I got angry then. Luke could sense it. Gully, too. He started fidgeting.

"There's rising damp behind the Wall of Woe," I announced. "You want to lift up the carpet and check out the floorboards?"

"Nah, that's okay." He winked at me. "You're Sky, right? I knew your mother."

"She set you on fire?" I turned to serve another customer. Steve Sharp stayed where he was. When there was space again, he caught my eye.

"Pass us that?" He nodded to Patti Smith's *Easter* from the Rocky and Otis buy. I'd forgotten about it, and Dad had priced it and put it on the back wall—land of sweet deals and raries. Luke gave Steve the record. He flipped the cover, peeked inside. A puzzled dent marked his brow like a tiny arrow pointing down. "This is mine, but I didn't sell it in."

I started to sweat. Here it was: the reason why Rocky and Otis didn't know about "Wishing Well"—the records were never theirs to begin with.

"How do you know it's yours?" I asked, stalling.

Steve Sharp tilted his head. "You always know your babies."

"Your son sold it in," Luke told him.

For a second everything stopped. Then Steve Sharp flashed his superwhites.

"That's right. I forgot." He gave Patti two taps on her hairy armpit and passed her back. I could tell he was rattled, though, and it gave me some satisfaction. He went to leave, adding stiffly, "Get your dad to call me. Tell him, no hard feelings."

I studied my palms, intent, like I was reading my future. I didn't look back up until I was sure he had gone.

Gully put on Elvis doing "Kentucky Rain." Then he lifted the cover of *Easter* and looked inside as Steve Sharp had. He snorted. "That man does *not* love records."

"What do you mean?" I asked.

"I mean he's marked them. A person who marks their records has no respect. It's a hate crime against vinyl."

We all peered into the cardboard cave. On the inside back there was a symbol. I knew it and Luke knew it. Three straight lines, like a primitive rake. Same as the symbol on Mia's tape. Same as the symbol on Nancy's. I was stunned silent. Luke was too. I flashed on Steve Sharp scooping tapes out of Elvis's tray like they were complimentary mints. So many times.

Gully *chh*ed his fist. "Excuse me—what's going on?"

We muttered, "Nothing."

"I can help, you know. I'm an excellent detective."

"You stick to the Bricker."

"And the Snouters," Gully added cheerily.

Luke sat hunched on the stool. He gave me a look that said, *Later* . . . We waited until Dad was back from lunch. Then Luke made an excuse to leave, and after a few minutes I did the same.

FALLEN ROBINS

I LED LUKE THROUGH the knotty backstreets to Ray's cottage. We hung back, planning. The water in the canal had receded almost to nothing; her murky sides were on display. Luke plucked spider grass. "You think we just ask him straight out?"

"I don't know. Ray's unpredictable. I don't think he'll admit that Mia was staying at his house—it opens up too much." I paused. "We should concentrate on Nancy. She can at least tell us where the tape came from. We can go from there."

Ray took a while to open the door. I was shocked by his appearance. He was wearing the kimono—untied. I was grateful that his huge stomach obliterated his tackle. But his skin! I was nearly blinded by the pink and white, the muzzy drifts of hair and edema. And his face! A rash cauliflowered his cheeks. He leaned back against a pile of books and tied his belt.

"She's not here. She didn't come home again. I'm in a complete state." He looked past me to Luke. "Who's he?"

Luke stepped up. "I'm Luke. Mia Casey was my sister."

Ray's eyes raced. He started to close the door on us, but Luke got a foot in.

"You can't just front up," Ray bleated. "I didn't do anything! Nancy owes me rent. She hasn't done the shopping or the cleaning. I'm living on dried fruit."

"I just want to talk," Luke said. "Did she stay here? My sister?"

Ray let go of the door. He was wheeling around his hallway. His kimono had become untied again, and this time he didn't fix it. He was pantomiming. "Ask Ray. Ray will help. Need some money or a place to crash? Ray's good for it. He won't ask questions." He snarled. "You're all the same. Take take take. But when is someone going to do something for *me*?"

Luke cast me a let's-get-out-of-here look, but I went in, dodging Ray's flubbing form. "I left something in Nancy's room." Ray was breathing heavily, the sound like industrial machinery. My eyes slid left to the stairs. I took them, fast.

Nancy's bedroom was the usual mess of books and clothes. I made a beeline for the boom box. The mix tape was still in there. I pressed play, and the music roared out of the speakers.

I scanned the room. My eyes lit on the collage on Nancy's cupboard, then past it to its ornate brass handles. They were definitely the same. Mia *had* been here. She had taken that photo *here* in this room. The boom box played "The Crying Game," the guitar sounding like two cats squalling in an alley. A feeling came over me that was thick and hot and formless. I ejected the tape and stuffed it in my pocket, and then I ran back down the stairs. Ray pressed his bulk against the door. Luke was on the other side of it.

Ray was too big to pass, but when he saw me, he latched on to my arm, and Luke was able to foist the door open. Ray's fingers needled for just a second, and then he let go with a queer smile. Luke grabbed me and we ran together until there was enough distance between us and Ray.

Luke leaned on his knees, catching his breath. He looked up at me, his eyes flashing. "Why'd you do that? I was about to break the door down."

I considered him, all gangly hesitance, and arched an eyebrow. My stomach was jittering like mad. Then I held out Nancy's tape. Luke held it against Mia's tape.

"Nancy says if a guy gives you a mix tape, it's True Fucking Love."

Luke made a face. "Steve Sharp?"

I remembered Vesna's talk about "the woo." What if the tapes were Steve Sharp's tools of seduction? And what had Nancy said about working an angle? It wasn't unbelievable that she should be shagging Steve Sharp and Otis Sharp at the same time. It wasn't unbelievable, it was just creepy.

Luke and I walked along the canal to the wall where Mia hung. We sat with our backs against her and stared at the water. After a while I took out my phone and texted Nancy.

Need to see you. Call me!

Where was she? With Otis? Or Steve? Or someone else entirely? What if I never saw her again? I felt a lump in my throat. Maybe our friendship had always been hollow. I'd needed someone to admire, and Nancy needed to be admired. And now that the framework had changed, we were all at sea.

"Well," I said, closing my palm over my phone. "I know where we can find her. If she's still with Otis, she'll be at the mess."

Luke nodded. He looked at me. I couldn't read his expression. He said, "You don't have to do all this, you know?"

"All what?"

"This . . . investigation."

"Ah, but I do. It's in my blood."

We staggered our return to the shop. I headed straight for the stereo, rewound Nancy's tape, and pressed play. The tracks were the same as the ones on Mia's tape. I knew the songs not just because I worked in a record store, but because they were a certain vintage. Dad nodded along. When "Wishing Well" sounded, he jolted to attention.

"Whose tape?"

"It's just a mix," I replied.

"Someone's got good taste," Dad said grudgingly.

A MINUTE'S SILENCE

ON THE LAST DAY of school Quinn cornered me in the girls' bathroom and asked if I wanted her to sign my dress.

"Go crazy," I said. "I'm not coming back next year."

"What do you mean?"

"We're moving. We're crossing the water. Newport."

"For real? Well, that sucks. It's only taken me three years to find a compadre and now you're absconding. . . . Are you happy?"

"I'm happy we're not moving to the country."

She nodded and was quiet for a bit. We listened to the last day's sounds: girls gone wild, shrieks and water bombs, the triumphant clang of emptied locker doors. Quinn brandished her Sharpie.

"Okay, bend over."

I bent over. I wriggled under the nib. Quinn was writing for a long time—on my shoulder blades and my spine and the soft spot above my hips. Finally she put the cap back on and sat on one of the toilets and lit a cigarette.

"What did you write?" I twisted to try to see.

"You'll have to take it off to read it." She smiled through the smoke. The words felt like a challenge, but I was up for it. I pulled my dress up over my head and stood there in my undies and singlet with my non-chest out on display. Quinn checked me out shamelessly. "I think it's cool that you don't wear a bra. I wish I didn't have to."

"You don't," I said, though she definitely did.

"I'm going to burn it."

I laughed as I spread my dress out on the bench.

Quinn had drawn a map.

"What is this?"

"That's where the mess is. Christmas Eve." She really was trying to burn her bra. She poked the cups with her cigarette. It caught and sent off a sharp smell as my fingers traced the line of the canal. Quinn hung her flaming bra on one of the dress hooks. "The password's 'Ringo.'" The smoke alarm sounded and a limp spray shot down from the ceiling. I threw my dress back on and we ran out laughing. We headed for the library and logged into Goldmine, where I nearly wet myself anyway because every record we'd listed had sold.

"Result!" I cried, and promptly printed off the list.

"You gonna show your dad?" Quinn asked.

"Uh-huh."

"Can I come?"

"Uh-huh."

Friday night family fish and chips. Quinn was eye-balling Luke over her potato cakes. She knew all about him now, knew that he was Mia's brother, and my boyfriend, but she didn't let on.

Meanwhile, the shop was in chaos. Records stuck out all over like country teeth. The bargain bins had been well plundered. The trestle table out front was caving under the pressure of 101 *Top of the Pops* records. But we had living, breathing, walking-around-eating customers. The Grand Sale was having a moment, and it made Dad merry enough to study my list of Goldmine results with minimal freak-out.

"Where did you get the stock?" he asked.

Quinn jumped in. "My grandma. In Sydney. She died. She had eclectic taste."

"I'm sorry," Dad said. "Not about the records, obviously—they're fucking great—but about your grandma."

"It's okay." Quinn smiled innocently. "I didn't really know her."

"So you just list them and choose a starting price?" Dad marveled. "It's incredible."

"It's not new, Dad." I rolled my eyes, but I felt a warm buzz inside. Something had shifted. Bill the Patriarch was finally getting it.

Later when Luke and Quinn and I had escaped to the roof, she said, "Your dad is a time traveler."

"Yeah, only he never goes forward."

"I'd go forward," Quinn decided.

"I'd go back," Luke said.

Quinn had her camera with her. She leaned over the rail and took a photo of the poster of Mia. It had been weeks since Luke had first put her up, and she was starting to look a little tired.

"That's her, huh?" Quinn said softly.

"That's her," Luke said.

"I didn't know her."

"I'm starting to think no one did."

"At least you had her for a while," Quinn said. "The thing about being an only child, you don't know your place in the world." She paused, and cocked her head, like she was tuning in some other frequency. When she tuned back into us, her eyes and voice was sharp. "If we go to the mess, you can talk to Otis."

"I heard he's a delicate flower," Luke said. "But I'm gonna try."

Quinn looked at Luke through her lens. She took a photo. "What's a good memory of her?" Luke closed his eyes. His words felt like a cool wind blowing across us.

"Remember I told Gully about the kid who wanted to fight me? Mia used to take me to the kung fu movies. One day, after, we ended up in the same ice cream parlor—me and Mia and the kid and his parents. I'd never told her who he was, but Mia knew just by the look on my face. She dumped a double scoop of rainbow and choc-mint in his lap. She said it's always better to do something, even if it turns out to be the wrong thing. Because no one ever got anywhere by sitting still."

We gazed at Mia's face, gave her a minute of silence. So much had happened since the first time I saw her. Her mouth that I'd once thought haughty looked soft now. Had she laughed a lot? Had she loved anybody? Did she know that Christmas Eve when she put on her flower crown and silver dress and headed out the door that she wouldn't be coming home? In my mind she merged with Nancy. She was smiling, saying, "It was just an accident, little sister. Just bad luck. Don't you know it has to end this way for some people?" I knew she was right, but that didn't mean I had to like it.

THE WORLD IS A TERRIBLE PLACE

MY PHONE—ALWAYS PRIZED, a symbol of friendship, of freedom—took on a new importance. I kept it on hand and waited for the magic ring. No Nancy, no Nancy, no Nancy. Saturday afternoon I saw her stroll past the shop like a stranger, like she'd never sat up on the back counter and teased Dad or me or Gully. I left my post and followed her down Blessington Street to the corner of the park. It was a perfect day, and the green was ringed with travelers. They came from all over, fixing their campervans in the last remaining strip of deregulated parking. As I turned to avoid a juggling crusty, I saw something else: Gully ducking behind a palm tree. For the moment I forgot my pursuit of Nancy and felt my way around the trunk. He was pressed against it; eyes shut, like if he couldn't see me, then I couldn't see him.

"Gully—what are you doing?"

One eye opened, then the other. "I thought you might need backup."

"Well, I don't." I craned my head past a circle of people who were taking turns laughing stupidly loud. "Shit—now she's gone."

"Mouth," Gully shot back. Then: "She's over there."

Sure enough, Nancy had stopped at the end of the playground.

"Nancy!" I shouted.

She turned but either didn't see me or didn't want to see me. She started walking off. I nudged Gully back in the direction of the Wishing Well. And then I dashed past the laughing club, trying to shake off the feeling that I was making them laugh louder.

Nancy ambled. She was carrying a hippie bag that had sheafs of paper sticking out of it. Her hair looked like she'd brushed it with a fork. I caught up with her, laying my hand on her arm, and she whipped around. When she saw it was me, her mouth dropped open, but the laugh never came. "Dollbaby," she said. "Are you stalking me?"

"Yes!" I willed her to smile. Her mouth didn't move. I hung around her. That was how it felt. I was *hanging*. And as it became clear that she wasn't going to talk to me, I clamped my feet to the ground, as if to earth us both.

"So . . . where are you going?"

Nancy shifted. "The beach. I'm meeting Otis."

"How is it going with him?"

She gave me a dull look and didn't answer. I broke then, and I couldn't keep the whine out of my voice. "I've been calling you and calling you."

"I lost my phone."

"I went to your place."

"I'm not staying there."

"I know that."

Nancy wrinkled her nose. She looked itchy to leave. I kicked a little dirt over her feet.

"Don't you wear shoes anymore?"

She dropped her cold pose and looked me in the eye. There was sadness there; it was unnerving. She said, "I wish I hadn't told you."

I tried to act diffident. "It doesn't change anything."

"Liar." She turned away. "Whatever."

I grabbed her arm.

"I wanted to ask you about the tape. The one that was in your bedroom. The mix tape with the Millionaires . . ." I rushed on. "Mia Casey had a tape too, with the symbol on it. You know—the three lines."

Nancy blinked. Her mouth slowly curled upward.

"Look at you, Nancy Drew. I thought Gully was the detective in the family."

"Luke has this photo of Mia. It was taken in your room—it's the same door handle. . . ."

Nancy quacked her free hand and rolled her eyes. "All that talk is just a whole lot of noise in the wrong place." A quote from somewhere.

I persisted. I was almost going to go the pretzel hold, but Nancy pulled her arm free. Papers fell from her bag and littered the street. She huffed and bent to pick them up. They were travel brochures, too many of them, to all different places.

"What's the matter with you?" Nancy snapped as she gathered the brochures. "So Mia had the same tape and she stayed in the same room—so what? So Ray's a sleaze. Your dad's girlfriend could have told you that. Mia's dead, Sky. She drowned. The world is a terrible place. End of."

She marched off so fast and forcefully that dust flew up. At Beach Road she turned back to see if I was still following, but I was done with that. I thought of the most hurtful thing I could say and then I shouted it.

"You're never going to get overseas. You're not going anywhere!"

I walked back feeling shaky and grim. When I turned onto Blessington Street, I saw a huddle outside the Wishing Well—Dad, Gully, Luke, some tourists— they were all out in front of the shop. As I drew closer, I heard whoops of excitement: Gully. He was running in tight circles, his hand tracing madly, and if he was aware of his audience, he didn't show it. Dad covered the open doorway, and Luke was under his plane tree, a smile lighting his face. When Gully saw me, he gave me a wide joker's grin and then reverted to superserious. A furrow appeared between his eyebrows. He touched his night vision goggles compulsively.

"We found the Jeep!" He was trying to keep his business face on. "We have *plates*! OWT 654. Constable

Eve Brennan's going to run them, and then we'll have a *name* and then, Agent Skylark, then I'll have my collar." He whirled around and told the tourists, "Move on, please, there's nothing to see." He sighed and said to himself, "A momentous day. Mo-ment-ous! *Chh!*"

Memo #5

Memo from Agent Seagull Martin
Date: Saturday, December 20
Agent: Seagull Martin
Address: 34 Blessington St., St. Kilda,
upstairs

STATUS UPDATE

POINT THE FIRST:

On Saturday, December 20, at
approximately 16:43 I, Agent Detective
Seagull Martin, Special Investigations
Unit, witnessed the white Jeep involved in
the Bricker case. I was sitting at my post
out in front of Bill's Wishing Well when
the Jeep passed by. Though it was too fast
for me to see the driver, CCTV revealed
the license plate.

POINT THE SECOND:

The license plate is OWT 654. I can
confirm the white Jeep has a sticker that
says LOVE LIVE LOCAL. The driver was
a male, Caucasian. He could have been
anywhere between 18 and 25. He wore
black sunglasses and had an overlarge

forehead. NB: ordinarily this is indicative
of a high intelligence quotient. My hunch
is this case is the exception to the rule.

POINT THE THIRD:
On the advice of Constable Eve Brennan,
SKPD, I have not actioned a stakeout.
Constable Brennan has informed her
supervisor, and I await the driver's ID.

On a personal note I'd like to commend
myself for having faith, patience, and
foresight. An arrest is imminent. I can feel
it in my waters!

EVERYBODY HATES NANCY

SATURDAY BECAME SUNDAY BECAME Monday, Tuesday, Wednesday. The shop kept me busy. We experienced a rash of sellers, hustling last-minute Christmas cash. Dad took a step back from the counter and put the Buys Book in my hand. "I bequeath you," he said with an ironic bow. I selected stock with Goldmine in mind. I did it all perfectly: the poker face, the fast flick. I was sensitive but not too sensitive. I had found my calling, just as the doors were closing. Settlement was set for the end of February. We had the summer, and after that, anything was possible. That was what I told Gully. I was determined to be jolly.

We, the Martins, were crap at Christmas. Thank Bob for late-night shopping. After we finally kicked out the last stragglers on Christmas Eve, Dad hauled out the old tree from the cupboard under the stairs. It was an el cheapo number made of white wire and tinsel; its branches were scanty and bent out of shape. We had kept all of Gully's primary school decorations: the glitter leaves and macaroni stars and the focus puller—a nativity set constructed entirely from toilet rolls. Dad drank ginger tea by the gallon. He put on the Tijuana Brass's swinging version of "God Rest Ye Merry Gentlemen," and we gathered around the tree, admiring the crap and tack. Dad put one arm around Gully and the other arm around me. "This is the last Christmas we'll have here. Let's make it a good one."

Gully *chh*ed his fist. "Roger that."

It was a cozy scene, but my mind kept fleeing. The mess was upon us. The mess, the mess! I had the map memorized. I had Quinn's ETA. In minutes Luke would be waiting for me under the plane tree.

I waited until Dad had put away his pudding. "Can I go to Quinn's for carols by candlelight?"

"You hate carols," Dad said.

"I hate *regular* carols. Quinn's are like anti-carols." I could feel Gully studying me, trying to catch me in a lie. I kept my body straight and my hands balled. If he could tell I was lying, he let it go.

"Where does she live?" Dad asked. "How are you going to get there?"

"Windsor. Luke's going to walk me."

"Luke? Our Luke?"

"Agent Casey, FBI." Gully's eyes were narrowed to slits.

"Yes," I huffed. "He's meeting me out front. Like, now."

Dad's face hollowed, and then he puffed his cheeks in a display of fatherly concern. He threw his hands up. "Okay."

Gully followed me out to the living room.

"What are the specs?"

"What do you mean?"

He gave me a long look. "Agent Sky, I can be discreet."

I studied his face; it was smart but forlorn. It was the face of the kid who never got picked for anything. I turned my attention to the presents under the tree. Dad had rewrapped Gully's night vision goggles, and there was something there for me from Mum, and also the obligatory shortbread from Vesna.

"Sky, Sky, Sky." Gully's face alternated green and red under the Christmas lights. "Is it about the Bricker? Or the Snouter?"

I paused for drama. "It's bigger than both of them."

Luke and I walked fast and silent, holding hands. I couldn't shake the feeling that we were being followed, but when I did the trick-stop-and-whirl-around, the view was always clear. Clouds hid a fingernail moon. Across the road the sea looked like a sleeping giant.

On Beach Road we counted the house numbers down, stopping finally in confusion.

"There's nothing here," Luke said.

"Don't be so sure." I searched my mental map of Quinn's map. This was the place, I knew it.

We faced a construction site, a concrete castle protected by a high wire fence. There was a display unit—

its window lit up like a school diorama. Luke and I took in the model of La Mer—fifty-five villas, plus restaurant and spa complex for discerning retirees. INVEST NOW! SELLING FAST! It was hard to imagine the future dream against the work in progress. ANOTHER URBAN RENEWAL ACHIEVEMENT, the sign read. The connection only made me more certain that we were in the right place.

We walked the length of the site and turned down a side street. The wind dropped. The surrounding houses were all stately homes, the kind with ancient hedges and German Shepherds. If I closed my eyes, I could hear the distinct hum of money.

At the end of the development lay an access road. Down there the air changed. I could no longer smell the sea, just cement and smoke. The occasional car rumbled in the distance, but an undertow was now discernible, a thud-thud-thud of music. I turned another corner and stumbled into a body. The body was at the end of a line of bodies disappearing through a break in the fence. Luke squeezed my hand hard. When we reached the front of the line, a torch shone in my face.

"Password?"

"Ringo."

And we were in.

This was the maze that led to the mess. We turned corners and went upstairs and downstairs—up, down, around, and all the while the music grew louder and the smoke sharper. Then we were in the bowels of the building, the future underground car park and I was so nervous and excited that it was all I could do to just breathe, and take the sensations as they hit, the odd flashes of light, the moving shadows, the air of intensity so thick you could carve distress signals into it.

The mess was people and oil-drum fires and music. Images flickered off and on various walls—snaps from Otisworld. There was something so self-conscious about it: people at a party watching pictures of people at a party.

Someone poked me. I twisted to see Quinn. She grappled me in a bear hug, her camera sticking into my chest. I came out of the hug and put my hand over my face like she was the paparazzi. She snapped me anyway.

"Have you seen Nancy?" I shouted above the music.

Quinn pointed to a pile of pallets and shouted back, "Otis is starting soon!"

I checked for familiar faces. Trilby saw me and swung his stethoscope from his fingers like a pendulum. Luke was staring at the pictures; his face looked sad. I guess he was waiting for Mia to crop up. I hoped that she wouldn't—not the photo I'd seen. I grabbed his hand and led him away from the flashing images. We tried to get the lay of the land, skirting the edges. There were candles everywhere. The walls looked like they were breathing.

Nancy was on an upper level, on a concrete island that looked like it was suspended in space. A narrow ladder led down to the makeshift stage. She wasn't alone up there. I glimpsed scarves and lanky rock legs, Rocky's solid quiff, and Otis's luminous face. Even from where I was standing, Nancy didn't look right. Otis had his sharkskin back turned to her, and Nancy was berating it. She threw a limp punch. And then she climbed down the ladder. I went to meet her at the bottom.

Nancy's face softened when she saw me. She started talking as if we'd already been talking. It took me a while to catch up.

Her voice was tough, but her eyes didn't match it. "What do you know? He fucking reneged. He said he was going to pay for my ticket. Bullshit." She shrugged, her whole body flopping with the movement. "I suppose he would have worked it out eventually."

I guessed she meant Steve Sharp. She drank from her flask, waggling it in her fingers. I could tell by the angle that it was almost empty. Nancy continued, her voice whiny. "Sky, I don't want there to be bad feelings between us. I'm always running from the bad feelings. Everybody hates Nancy."

"I don't hate you. I'm worried about you."

"You don't have to worry about me." But as she said it, her eyes darkened. She stared at a group of scarf girls dancing; her face turned hard. "Otis is sweet, but his dad is a pig."

"Why'd you do it, then?"

"Because he's got a big dick and a lot of money." She laughed. I was pretty sure she was quoting. I wanted to tell her she didn't have to, but she'd drifted off to dance. Under the pulsing lights she looked unreal. "Dance with me," she called back. I moved limply, feeling awkward, wanting escape. Then suddenly she stopped.

"He's starting."

Otis and crew were climbing down the ladder. Otis was wearing his fox head. He knocked it a couple of times on the way down, which made it look more comic than surreal. Otis the fox, Rocky the duck, and the drummer had some kind of rodent head happening, but when I saw the bass player, my mouth went dry—he was wearing Gully's snout.

I scanned for Luke or Quinn in the sea of shifting bodies, and that was when I saw a figure smaller than most, a midget in night vision goggles, hand aloft, tracing the air. "Gully!" I shouted, and pushed through bodies like pillars until I reached him. I pulled him into a hug. I could feel his heart hammering.

"What are you doing here? How did you get in?"

"Stealth." Gully smirked beneath the goggles. "This is a weird party." He was looking around and then he stopped. He must have seen the snout because he extracted himself and started moving forward. He was slippery-quick, too fast for me. And then someone else was moving after him. Luke. But Gully weaved and Luke kept getting blocked. I watched Gully climb onto the stage, over to the bass player to reclaim his property. The bass player let him. Gully returned to the crowd. I made my way toward him, wading through strangers. By now Luke was up and aiming for Otis. Rocky—ever steroided—turned to attack. The drummer started up—what did he know? Maybe the mess was supposed to go like this and he didn't get the memo—but after a few beats he held his sticks aloft, and then there was nothing but the ringing quiet and open-mouthed mess-heads staring at something about to happen.

Luke punched Otis, straight in the jaw. Otis dropped like a sack of spuds. One minute he was up, the next he was down. It was like the punch to start the end of the world. Rocky set on Luke. They grappled around the pallets, finally crashing into the newly abandoned drum kit. The snoutless bass player was crouching, hiding his head behind his instrument. Mess-heads stormed the stage, and the scarf girls bent over Otis's prone body, guarding him fiercely. I was at the foot of the chaos, holding tight to Gully, who had his hands over his ears. Someone had put the music back on, but it was crackling, fragmenting, and the broken sounds were like a mirror of the scene. Where had Luke gone? He and Rocky could have rolled out to sea, for all I knew, because the lights were shorting along with the sounds.

In all the hubbub I had forgotten about Nancy. In a flash I saw her, climbing the rickety ladder, swaying slightly above the masses.

She climbed up and up. All I could do was watch her.

Then there was a loud crack. The generator seized and the room went dark—the only light left came from fires and camera flashes. Gully primed his night vision goggles. He raised his hand in the classic survivor fist. "Everybody stay calm!" But something was rising above even Gully: sirens and the word rushing like a bad wind. *Cops! COPS!*

I froze as figures bolted into the black. Then more figures entered with lights and nightsticks. I backed into a corner, letting go of Gully. The generator juddered back to life and somebody screamed.

Nancy. She wavered on the platform, eight feet up, her toes fairly curling over the edge, her head hanging, her hair mushrooming. And then she was falling and Gully was running toward her with his arms out, going for the big save. They both went down. There was a stunned silence, and then Gully's voice rose up. "I'm okay! I'm okay!" A hand came up from under Nancy's body. It was waving a pig snout.

"IN THE JAILHOUSE NOW"

WAY TO KILL A party, dude."

That was Rocky. I'd ended up next to him in the roundup. He was stuffed into the tightest pair of pants I'd ever seen. I was surprised he could breathe, let alone bitch. Luke was on the other side of the room, next to Otis, both of them bleeding. Otis's eye looked like mashed turnip. Luke's lip had gone bee-stung. I clocked Quinn. She had her camera at her hip and was surreptitiously sneaking shots. I didn't recognize anyone else. Most people's masks had slipped, faces showing fear and worry and regret.

The police sorted through us, checking ID, searching bags, weeding out the underagers. I blew into the tube, thankful I hadn't drunk anything.

"That's my brother," I told the officer, pointing to Gully, who was only just taking off his night vision goggles. "Can I sit with him, make sure he's okay?"

"All night long at the police station," she quipped.

Boys and girls went in separate police vans. I jostled to get next to Quinn.

"Did you drink?" she whispered.

"No."

"What about you?"

She shook her head.

"What happens now?" I asked.

"They'll call our folks. They might charge us. They'll try and charge someone." She stopped to take a picture. Heads turned at the sly click. "I think we'll be out for Christmas."

"What will your mum do?"

"Ground me. Take my computer away. What about your dad?"

I thought about it. "I don't know."

"What was Gully *doing*?"

"Saving Nancy."

At the police station we were hustled off to holding cells. There was a bag lady, a working girl, and a fancy-pants lady who must have been in by mistake. She couldn't stop crying. Nancy and Gully weren't with us, and for a long time I was too intimidated to talk to the guard. I sat next to Quinn and tried to close my senses. Luke, Otis, and Rocky were in the cell opposite with mess-heads and rough nuts; in the corner an old bum was curled up like a cat. Luke and Otis had given up glowering at each other. Luke stared at nothing. Rocky and Otis mumbled to each other and after a while not even that.

One by one the mess-heads and deviants were released until the only faces I recognized belonged to Rocky and Otis and Luke and the bum. The bum began to sing, his voice gruff but tuneful, and then I recognized both the singer and the song. It was the Fugg, doing "In the Jailhouse Now." Otis sat with his arms folded and a flat look on his face. Slowly he began tapping his foot to the Fugg's song, and then he joined in, harmonizing, in his distinctive, hiccupy yawl. Rocky brought his head out of his hands. He relaxed; his big forehead went baby-skin smooth. The Fugg sang in an old-timey way that gave me memory creaks and good shivers. Even the weeping woman in my cell stopped to blow her nose. I exchanged a glance with Luke. For the first time since we'd been in, he smiled. Things were going to be okay. I could feel it.

"Martin?" they called. I stood up; my bones were aching. "Somebody loves you." I stayed where I was, not understanding what he meant, until he unlatched the door. "You can go."

Dad and I walked out of the police station and into his car without a word between us. The moon was clear now, the clouds all gone. He turned the key. I opened the window and inhaled freedom.

He parked at the back of the shop. He cut the engine and lowered his head to the steering wheel. Then he lifted it again and turned to me. "You okay?"

I nodded. The engine was ticking as it cooled down.

It was a comforting sound, signifying a changing state. I wanted to lose myself to it. "How's Gully?"

"He's fine. He's got a broken arm."

"Ouch," I mumbled. I knew Dad was waiting for an explanation, and that he deserved it.

"He followed me there," I said. "I didn't know. I would never take him somewhere like that. And the only reason I was there—" I stopped. My reason contained too much—my reason wouldn't fit in the car. My reason was Mia and Nancy and the teenage call to wildness and Luke's desperate need to know. And it was something to do with belonging, too, though I wouldn't work that out until later. I stared at Dad and I had nothing, but he just put his hand over mine.

"They're going to put Gully in the paper."

"Wow. He'll love that." I was quiet, wanting to ask, but not wanting to.

"Nancy's going to be fine too. She was lucky she was drunk, gave her a dead fall." He paused. "She has to wear a brace for a bit. A neck brace.

I nodded. Nancy in a neck brace. She'd probably find a way to make it look sexy. Dad's hand felt warm over mine. It made me feel small. He said, "What happened to you? You used to be a sweet kid."

The stink of the bins was creeping in. I cranked the window up. I felt like crying, and then I was.

"Hey, hey." Dad hugged the half of me he could get to. It was the first time I could remember him smelling like himself, not of grog and defeat, but warm, musty, kind of like his T-shirt could use a wash.

I said, "Remember you used to say Joe Meek had no place in the world? You said he had one foot in the past and the other in the future. Like he didn't fit anywhere. I feel like that sometimes. Even with you and Gully."

Dad hugged me harder. "You fit. You fit fine." He kept hugging. I almost couldn't breathe. Then he let go and I wiped my eyes—then rolled them—and snuffled and yawned.

"Come on," Dad said. "Agent Seagull Martin wants to debrief."

THE GRACE OF BOB

CHRISTMAS MORNING. LATE. OUTSIDE my window the world
was a soft, unruffled blue, but already the sun
was pressing upon its edges. I lay back in bed and
closed my eyes, enjoying the quiet, my mind parade:
the mess. The raid. Nancy falling. Gully's hand with
the snout raised high. Otis and the Fugg's jailhouse
jamboree. Luke's last smile. Luke! I had no way of con-
tacting him. I wondered if he was going to turn up for
lunch. Had Otis told him anything? Did it make a difference? I felt different. When I looked at the picture
of Mia, I felt sadness but also a sense of finality. I felt
lighter. Even when I thought about the shop and the
future. Even when I thought about Mum.

I got dressed and knocked on Gully's door. He was
struggling to put his T-shirt on over his cast. After I'd
sorted him, I looked up and around. The evidence wall
was on the way out. The Polaroids were gone, the string
and star stickers.

The smallness of St. Kilda: it turned out that white
Jeep was registered to one Rocco Cipriani, aka Rocky.
Some random mess-head had swiped Gully's pig snout

and flung it onstage at Luna Park. Some bands get underpants, Otis got animal masks. Constable Eve Brennan put the eyes on Rocky, and he led her to the mess and the rest was history.

Gully's cast was pristine.

"Can I be the first one to sign it?" I asked.

He nodded. "No swear words!"

I held the Sharpie over the cast, and my mind went blank. I wanted to write something profound. It seemed to me that the cast was the culmination of all of Gully's work and to just write "Get Well Soon" would be an insult.

"I have to think about it. Does it hurt?"

"It's itchy. But injuries make great covers: casts, crutches, mouthguards, eye patches . . ."

I smiled. "So it's all good?"

"Affirmative."

"Did you remember to wrap Dad's present?"

Gully nodded to his desk; the bulky package waited. It looked more like a football than a single.

"I used a lot of bubble wrap. Digital intel is useless."

Dad was tidying the living room. In other words, he had a big black plastic tub and was sweeping all manner of stuff into it: records and bills and magazines and crockery. "Merry Christmas!" he said, all jolly, pausing to plant kisses on our foreheads.

Gully brought the package around from his back. "This is from us. Sky found it and I wrapped it."

We held our breath as Dad began the excavation. His fingers found the single. "Well," he said softly. "Well. Look at that. Where did this come from?"

"Goldmine," I lied.

"Do you like it?" Gully asked.

Dad grinned. "Are you crazy?" He took the record out of its sleeve and put it on the player. The Millionaires filled the flat in all their wobbly, demented glory. I checked for Steve Sharp's mark inside the sleeve, but Gully had blacked over it. He saw me looking and gave me a sly thumbs-up. I returned it. Wishing Well was so familiar and yet every time I played it, I heard some little difference. A tell that could not be translated. Like Dad said, "There's a lot going on in there." I remember thinking, *If songs can be seen, then "Wishing Well" shimmers*. Right there in the living room for three minutes and four seconds, we, the Martins, were in exactly the right place.

"Item," Dad announced. "We have guests arriving at twelve hundred hours. I'm putting the turkey on."

Luke came first. His lip was still swollen, and his eyes held the promise of stories. Eve came second, with crackers and cake and elaborate mocktails. She kissed Dad and me and Gully and even Luke, who wasn't expecting it. I saw the color rise on his neck, but he was smiling. She'd brought presents, too: a copy of the *Police Gazette* for Gully and a crystal radio kit; a Body Shop basket for me and a book called *What Color Is Your Parachute?*

"I know," she said. "You're hard to buy for."

"Sky's a mystery," Dad agreed.

I had been wondering about Nancy. Would she come? Would I get to see the neck brace? I imagined myself cooing at her, *Neck braces are everywhere this season*. I didn't like the way we'd parted. I wanted to hear her donkey-honk laugh again. When the doorbell rang, Gully and I both leaped for it. We tramped downstairs and yanked the door open to find a man in a blue suit with the sun making a halo behind him.

It was the Fugg, but he didn't look like the Fugg. He was clean. His hair was oiled back, his beard trimmed and food-free; his hands clasped in front of his stomach looked pink and soft as baby voles. The Fugg's suit was a little small and moth-eaten. He'd teamed it with loafers (no socks—there was nothing he could do about the scabs on his ankles). He was carrying a green shopping bag. I braced myself for the clink of bottles that never came.

"Hor-doevers!" Dad announced in his posh voice.

Oh, the awkwardness of the starter! The Fugg sat opposite Luke at the table, and the two of them just looked at each other. Luke's face serious, the Fugg smiling at the tablecloth. Nancy's chair stayed empty. I couldn't look at Luke without wanting to kiss him, so I studied the Fugg. When he picked up his knife and fork, his hands shook so hard it made my heart wince. Gully was watching Dad's face carefully, and I wondered if his reason for inviting Ernst extended beyond charity. Something like a there-but-for-the-grace-of-Bob-go-I. Conversation was stilted. Dad laughed too hard at a non-joke and nearly choked on his vol-au-vent. Just before turkey time Gully popped Nancy's cracker, and after that I relaxed. This was Christmas: silly hats and sinking pavlova. The turkey that worked. Eve's mock-tails flowing like sweet, fizzy rivers. There was laugh-ter and food and music—the holy trinity—and when Lee Hazlewood sang, "Some velvet morning when I'm straight," Gully and I locked eyes and grinned. This was the first Christmas we'd seen Dad sober.

After lunch we spread out, leaning back in our chairs, bloated and happy. Sunlight bathed the kitchen table in a gentle haze. Eve told the one about the guy who found a cracker with a message in it that said, "Help! I'm trapped in the cracker factory!" Dad told the story of Chuck Berry throwing his rings into Sydney Harbor. Gully went on an extended ramble about Garbo, the world's most famous spy. I told the one about the blithe psychopath and the Hare Krishna's finger, but then Luke said he didn't have any stories and we all went quiet.

Dad cleared his throat. "Do you want to ring your parents, son?"

It was so strange to hear him say "son"—and even stranger to see Luke accept it.

Dispersion, television, cups of tea. At five the Fugg

made moving noises. He kissed Eve's hand and bowed to Dad. "I thank you." He gave Gully a monster hug and gripped my hands. He said: "I have become the thing-ness of all the things I've seen."

"Is that yours?" I asked.

The Fugg winked at me. "It's yours."

Later I wrote it on Gully's cast. It seemed right.

FADE AND BLOOM

FTER THE MESS, AFTER Christmas, after she'd moved out of Ray's and secured a fistful of traveler's checks, Nancy Cole, KGB, pushed her face against the window of the Wishing Well. It was late February and the signs that summer was ending were everywhere: gray mornings, where the sea rolled cold across the foreshore. Racks of cheap summer dresses dominated the strip. The leaves on the plane tree began to crack and curl. The Purple Onion disappeared overnight. The tourists still clung to the odd beach day, but the scent of tanning oil waned as the days grew shorter.

Nancy owled her eyes at the glass. I saw her looking straight at me. She gave me a sad sort of smile. I motioned that she should come in, but she shook her head, a swift, small shake that seemed like a waste of her glorious tresses. I put down *Record Collector*, picked up my bag, and went out to meet her. We moseyed down to the park and sat on the swings.

"No neck brace?" I asked, a smile slipping out.

"That old thing?" Nancy sniffed. "No, I'm good as

new. I'm going to get a business card that says 'traveling,' like Holly Golightly in *Breakfast at Tiffany's*." She lit a cigarette and blew a plume of smoke into the blue. "We had some adventures, didn't we?"

I pushed dirt around with the toes of my sneakers and didn't say anything. Nancy already looked far away, like someone I'd only known in a dream.

"How's Luke?" she asked.

"How's Otis?" I countered.

"Ha!" Nancy raised her eyes to the scudding clouds. "Gone the way of all things." She scrunched her face and put her hand out to stop my swing. "I wanted to say sorry. You were a good friend to me. I'll send you postcards." She paused. "I don't know why I am the way I am. I was thinking about it. I remember when I was little, the first time I ever heard the word 'opportunistic,' I thought, I want to be that. I didn't know it was a bad thing." She nodded and her face was as serious as I'd ever seen it. "I'm not bad, you know."

"I know," I said softly. "Yeah, we had some adventures."

Nancy started swinging, kicking her legs higher and higher. I swung again too. We were out of sync. Nancy went up when I went down. After a while I jumped off. I rooted around in my bag for paper and a pen and wrote down the Newport address. "Send the postcards here," I told her, and made my way back to the shop.

The campervans had gone; the feral travelers and laughing clowns had moved on, chasing the sun. I used to look at them and wonder what it would be like to just pick up and leave, to fade and then bloom somewhere else.

I was about to find out.

On the last day of February I was on the roof. I had swept up the cigarette butts and Dunlops caps, and I was putting Mum's records in a cardboard box. Out of habit I popped the opera glasses. It was early evening, and the parrots were shrieking from tree to tree. I looked at the green and the sea and the sky. Mia Casey was still on the wall, but she was looking a little worse for wear. Soon she'd be gone altogether. Dad and Gully and I had packed our lives into 237 cardboard boxes. All the memories and music and minutiae; the bits and scraps of our existence. Across the water the Newport house waited, along with a shop that was half the size of the Wishing Well and smelled like fresh paint. And promise.

The sun went down like a big eye closing. Down below the night people were coming out, all flashy earrings and cheap pashminas. And through the wind in the boat masts and the distant dogs barking, something else rose up.

"Sky, Sky, Sky, Sky!"

I looked down and saw three smiling faces: one cautious but crackable; one weathered and wry; one obscured by night-vision goggles. Luke and Dad and Gully. Gully was holding the fish and chips. I ran down to meet them. I was starving.

ACKNOWLEDGMENTS

THANKS TO MY FAMILY for love and music; to Namrata Tripathi and all at Atheneum for making my day (year!) when they decided to publish *Girl Defective*; to Jill Grinberg (and all at Jill Grinberg Literary) for keeping the faith; to Claire Craig for her early love of Sky and Gully; to Melita Granger, who provided support and wisdom and structural advice; and to my writerly friends, who remind me why it's all worth it. When I was eighteen, I dropped out of university and got a job in a record store; it was the best education I could have had. So thanks to Dixons, with a special shout-out to Sarah Carroll and Val Davis.

love this **book**?
ready for **more**?

pulseit
.com

read, heart **&** share
the newest teen books for **free!**

Listen: Travis Coates was alive once, and then he wasn't. Now he's alive again. Simple as that.

DON'T LOSE YOUR HEAD!

JOHN COREY WHALEY, author of the Printz and Morris Awards winner **WHERE THINGS COME BACK,** returns with a touching, hilarious, and wholly original new novel.

atheneum

PRINT AND EBOOK EDITIONS AVAILABLE
TEEN.SimonandSchuster.com

SOME TIMES WHEN YOU TRY AND ACT SMOOTH, YOU CAN REALLY END UP BLOWING IT.

CHECK OUT THESE GRIPPING STORIES FROM ACCLAIMED NEW AUTHOR *Jason Reynolds*:

"Reynolds is an author to watch."
—*School Library Journal* on *When I Was the Greatest*

"An unexpectedly gorgeous meditation on the meaning of family, the power of friendship, and the value of loyalty."
—*Booklist* on *When I Was the Greatest*

"A vivid, satisfying, and ultimately upbeat tale of grief, redemption, and grace."
—*Kirkus Reviews* on *The Boy in the Black Suit*

Discover the gritty world
of acclaimed author
E. R. FRANK.

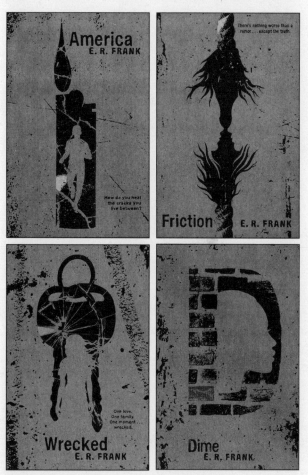

★"AN IMPORTANT WORK." —*School Library Journal* on **Dime**, STARRED REVIEW

★"A WRENCHING TOUR DE FORCE." —*Kirkus Reviews* on **America**, STARRED REVIEW

★"GRIPPING . . . UNSETTLING." —*Booklist* on **Friction**, STARRED REVIEW

"COMPULSIVELY READABLE." —*School Library Journal* on **Wrecked**

PRINT AND EBOOK EDITIONS AVAILABLE

From Atheneum Books for Young Readers | Teen.SimonandSchuster.com

SIMMONE HOWELL

is the award-winning author of *Notes from the Teenage Underground* and *Everything Beautiful*. Before becoming a writer, she studied literature and worked in secondhand bookstores and record shops. She lives with her husband and son and crazy dog in Melbourne, Australia. Visit her at simmonehowell.com.

THIS IS THE STORY OF A WILD GIRL AND A GHOST GIRL,
OF A BOY WHO KNEW NOTHING AND A BOY WHO THOUGHT
HE KNEW EVERYTHING.

IT'S A STORY ABOUT SKYLARK MARTIN, who lives with her father
and brother in a vintage vinyl shop and is trying to find her place in
the world. It's about ten-year-old Super Agent Gully and his case
of a lifetime. It's about beautiful, reckless, sharp-as-knives Nancy.
And it's about tragi-hot Luke and just-plain-tragic Mia Casey.
It's about the dark underbelly of a curious neighborhood.
It's about summer and weirdness and mystery and music.
*And it's about life and death and grief and romance. All the
good stuff.*

COVER DESIGN BY DEBRA SFETSIOS-CONOVER ■ COVER ILLUSTRATION COPYRIGHT © 2014 BY JEFFREY EVERETT ■ BACK PANEL PHOTOGRAPH
COPYRIGHT © 2014 BY HENRY BEER ■ ATHENEUM BOOKS FOR YOUNG READERS ■ SIMON & SCHUSTER ■ NEW YORK ■ AGES 14 UP ■ 0915
EBOOK EDITION ALSO AVAILABLE

Visit us at
TEEN.SimonandSchuster.com

ISBN 978-1-4424-9761-0   **$10.99** U.S./$12.99 Can.

51099

9 781442 497610